Ride a Godless Land

When Ash Carmody, Wes Shelby and Rand Malleroy ventured west to make Wagontown their home they were welcomed with open arms, for all three were recognized as exactly the fine upstanding type of newcomer that could make the town prosper.

But a secret shadow lay over the trio and the day the towering preacherman Doone arrived in town with blazing eyes and thonged-down Peacemakers, they knew their past had returned to haunt them.

Doone sought nothing but vengeance and, as his guns filled his hands as if by magic, he promised nothing but death.

Newcastle City Council

Newcastle Libraries and Information Service

☎ **0191 277 4100**

Due for return	Due for return	Due for return
2 9 DEC 2014		

Please return this item to any of Newcastle's Libraries by the last date
shown above. If not requested by another customer the loan can be
renewed, you can do this by phone, post or in person.
Charges may be made for late returns.

Ride a Godless Land

MATT JAMES

A Black Horse Western

ROBERT HALE · LONDON

© Matt James 2005
First published in Great Britain 2005

ISBN 0 7090 7848 X

Robert Hale Limited
Clerkenwell House
Clerkenwell Green
London EC1R 0HT

Typeset by
Derek Doyle & Associates, Shaw Heath.
Printed and bound in Great Britain by
Antony Rowe Limited, Wiltshire.

CHAPTER 1

HEADIN' WEST

'Holy Toledo! Look at 'em come!'

The excited cry that rang out along the crowded walks of the Mississippi River town was quickly swallowed by something louder and deeper – the clatter of a hundred straining shire horses and the rumble of the heavily laden Conestoga wagons which suddenly appeared at the head of the street, announcing that they had arrived at long last.

The Westbounders!

The City of Cairo had only just heard that the thaw to the east had at last melted the snow in the high passes which had kept the wagon trains locked in fast since late fall. Yet here they were already, hundreds and maybe even thousands of the folks who were responding that springtime to Horace Greeley's stirring exhortation to 'Go West, young man, go West!'

Not only young men had responded, as wide-eyed

5

city folks quickly realized. Wherever they looked they saw, rumbling by on wagons festooned with packrolls and furnishings, cooking utensils and bedrolls of a dozen gaudy hues, entire clans and families of hopefuls, ancient graybeards chewing their tobacco quids, toddle-aged kids in hand-me-downs and babes in arms, some born on the journey from the East, all hungry and eager for whatever the Great West had to offer.

And between the Westbounders and their dream land now, just the one final barricade.

Broad it lay, wide and swift and deep, the great father of waters, called the Mississippi.

Year after year it had rolled past the town with the same unchanging brown ugliness that had characterized its passage through centuries of redskin history, carrying Illinois trees, Iowa mud and something that had drowned in St Louis. By day it was a sullen challenge to anyone and everyone who attempted to cross. But Lady Night, friend as she was to lovers, thieves and owls, is kind to rivers also. By tonight, wide-eyed travellers originally intimidated by its swollen breadth would find that a Missouri moon and midwestern stars turned the Old Muddy into liquid silver and gold. The light of the oil-lamps burning on the western banks would reflect deeply on the moving surface, with busy ferries with bright running lights fore and aft lending their own brilliance, looking, from the Cairo shore, like fabled Eastern craft of the days of the *Arabian Nights.*

But the night was hours away, and long before

then the gritty reality of the historic day would be making itself felt all the way from Freedom Street to the water's edge.

For while many welcomed the invasion and the profits it would bring, there were just as many resentful and downright hostile towards so many aliens landing suddenly amongst them without so much as a by-your-leave.

The Dogwood Saloon hard by the docks was where trouble usually flared first during hard times. Or even simply when a certain class of Cairo citizenry might begin to feel their oats, their prejudices or simply the effects of all the cheap booze they were swallowing.

The drinkers and deadbeats mingling with the lowly paid levee hands were out in force on the biggest day in Cairo's history. But they weren't pleased or proud, not a single, surly one of them.

'Just look at 'em,' sneered a day laborer who worked for the cattle companies, as a little family went by the grimed windows. 'Pasty-faced towners, hill-billy gopher-hunters and Kentucky sodbusters! They're gonna open up the freakin' West? I'd laugh if it wasn't so loco.'

'The trash the East don't want they foist on us,' supported another.

'Only good thing is they ain't stayin', just passin' on through.'

'Yeah, that's if the Ol' Miss lets 'em,' growled a muscle-knotted docker, dragging his gaze away from the human traffic passing by.

'What ya mean, Olaf?' asked a companion.

The docker gestured northwards where a long dark stain was spreading across the afternoon sky.

'I'm meanin' there's gonna be rain by early night at the latest. Before mornin' she'll be too high-risin' for the cattle boats they got lined up to take them fools across.'

A companion grunted in agreement.

'The man's right, you know. The way she's been runnin' the last few days it'd only take a good spit to put her to the banks. But what loss anyway? Eh, boys?'

Heads nodded. Almost everyone was the enemy here, from Sheriff Buck Flory and his deputies to the wealthy merchants, the rivermen and the riders in from the ranches. This was their jealously guarded refuge from the endless list of people they feared, hated or suspected. Curiously, the newcomers seemed to sense this as they continued drifting by the sagging swinging doors, until suddenly the pattern changed and three from the wagons came striding in together, signalling to the barkeep for beers.

Silence fell but the newcomers didn't seem to notice as they strode confidently to the bar. Although unalike in general appearance, there was a kind of uniformity about the trio none the less. Each was tall and youthful-looking and was dressed more like a businessman or even levee boss than an honest-to-God levee-loafer or saloon layabout.

When they began talking, keen ears picked up something even more highly suspicious than their appearance. They heard Northern vowels, an absence of the familiar Southern drawl.

'So, who kicked the trash-can over, boys?'

The trio fell silent to stare curiously at the scar-faced man who'd spoken. Only then did they realize they were the cynosure of every eye. They traded glances, straightened, then shot a look at the batwings. Before they could leave, a young tough, old and battered before his time, moved before the doors and hooked thumbs in his belt, tough-guy fashion.

'North, right?' he demanded.

'So?' replied the tallest of the three.

'Guess we can take that as a yes, eh, boys?'

The newcomers were no longer interested in their drinks. They'd only met up during the trek and as yet had no real experience of the true West. Yet they were savvy enough to sense they'd walked into the wrong place at the wrong time.

They traded quick glances and were headed for the doors when the husky day-laborer stepped before them, halting them.

'It'll cost you to git out, Yankees,' he mouthed. 'I mean, really cost after what you bluecoats done to us in the war. . . .'

'The war?' the youngest interloper said. 'That was over years ago.'

'You wish!' the bruiser said with sudden anger, and threw a roundhouse right for the jaw.

The newcomer ducked low out of harm's way, bobbed up and broke the bruiser's nose with his elbow. Within moments the quiet of the watering-hole was transformed into the roar and crash of a rafter-rattling brawl which eventually spilled out into the street, the racket carrying easily to reach the barred windows of the squat mud-brick building with the barely legible legend CAIRO SHERIFF'S OFFICE painted across the false-front.

The trio shook the hand of Sheriff Buck Flory in turn. Each Westbounder showed visible signs of the ruckus they'd become involved in, were grateful to the stubby badgeman who had put an instant stop to the trouble simply by walking up and blasting off three above their heads. The law appeared remarkably calm and unfazed by it all.

'OK, OK,' Flory growled around a chewed-off stogie, 'you're happy I got there in time and I'm happy you're all getting on the boats tonight. Er, you are with the wagons and moving on, I take it?'

They nodded. The badgeman squinted at Flanagan in the background, then nodded and motioned everybody on their way. They didn't dally. Neither did the law. Flory then swung on the brawlers and began issuing on-the-spot five-dollar fines for disturbing the peace, then kicked the muscle-bound day-laborer in the knee when he made to object.

The man yelped and fell over. He was hauled erect by his companions and dragged away, leaving the sheriff with the suddenly peaceful stretch of dockside street all to himself.

Flory had his own way of doing things, prided himself that his methods, although frowned upon by some, guaranteed that he bossed a tolerably peaceful town; he took pride in the fact that there hadn't been a truly major crime in his area of jurisdiction in many months now.

He had no way of sensing that all this was about to change.

'One for the road, pards?'

'You mean one for the river, don't you?'

'One for the whatever. And one for you, Flanagan, you old worry-wart.'

Flanagan shook his head. He was a Kansan, heading home from a visit to the city, who'd hooked up with the three younger men from the train. He knew the river and was growing anxious.

The rain was sluicing down outside the place which bore the legend **Gin Sold Here** above its dark doors. The rugged blacksmith had made the Mississippi crossing several times and knew just how bad it could be when the floods came down. Of course, he knew he could just quit and get on board the loading cattle boat and leave his trio of new 'friends' to fend for themselves. Yet there was something about the three's enthusiasm and high spirits that seemed to arouse the protective instinct in him, so he downed his last one and gave it one more try.

'Boys, let me remind you what lies ahead and you'll see that mebbe you ain't cut out for—'

'We know what lies ahead,' said one, grinning.

'God knows they bored us silly with it often enough back in the snow passes. Seems by now we know every inch of the trail waiting for us when we cross.'

'Damn right,' agreed another, gazing at the smoky ceiling. 'Let me see now . . . Oh yeah – from Cairo due west through the southern hill-country of Missouri, then following roughly the border between Oklahoma and Kansas until the Cimarron is reached. From there, each of the seven wagon masters will strike out separately, leading the settlers to their various destinations—'

'Hell, even I know the rest, Ash,' broke in the junior of the three. 'Listen. North to Kansas and Colorado, north-west to Wyoming and Utah, south-west to New Mexico and Arizona or due west to Nevada and California or break off south to mighty Texas. How am I doing, old-timer?'

'You didn't mention the towns like El Paso, Denver, Wichita Falls, Pueblo and Cheyenne,' chimed in the serious one, rolling the romantic sounding names round his tongue. Then he paused. 'But . . . hey, all that sounds so good, mebbe we should heed Flanagan and get moving, just in case the river really floods up and we get stranded.'

They left 'Gin Sold Here' a short time later and Flanagan heaved a sigh of relief. They could hear the cattle-boat tooting its whistle through the rain, and the cold had a sobering effect. With Flanagan leading the way they covered several wind-lashed blocks before the blacksmith led them off down a winding short cut. The trio was following close behind, laughing and joshing when from an alleymouth hard by came the unmistakable sounds of violence: thuds, a cry of agony, a violent curse.

They propped to peer ahead through the gloom where writhing figures were dimly visible a hundred feet distant. Flanagan promptly veered away from the trouble before realizing that nobody was following him.

'What in damnation?' he shouted peevishly. 'What now?'

The three continued to stare off through the grey veils of rain gloom at the scene, which was dimly lit by the window light spilling from the squalid shacks flanking the dead-end laneway. The brawl appeared truly violent with straining grunts, curses and the scraping of boots. Flanagan shouted to his charges again, and drawing no response, retraced his steps to the mouth of the cul-de-sac where he couldn't help but look at the brutal drama being enacted before their eyes.

He opened his mouth to speak when a cry of mortal agony came from one of the fighters, a cry that rose to a scream before breaking off with chilling suddenness.

The man crashed to ground.

His attacker stood above him for a moment; the onlookers could hear the labored rasping of his breath.

'That man has been hurt!' gasped one. Then, before Flanagan could halt him, went striding into the laneway. 'Hey, you there. Hold up!'

Instantly the shadowy figure snatched up a satchel and darted into a flanking laneway to be quickly lost from sight. Next moment the three were sprinting forward, but by the time they reached the cross-alley which the man had taken, it was empty.

Flanagan, reluctantly trailing behind, said irritably:

'Damn it, it's only a street brawl. Are we goin' to miss the damned boat just because of a lousy, drunken—'

'He's hurt,' the tallest of the three said, and hurrying to the downed figure, dropped on one knee by his side. Then: 'No, by glory – he's dead!'

Dead he certainly was. There was no question of this even in the semi-darkness. A bearded man, tall and rugged and dressed like a miner, he lay on his back with his head resting on the steps of a lighted hovel. The haft of a big knife protruded from his chest, the surrounding ground was soaked in blood.

'Good God!' Flanagan gasped in horror. 'The poor devil never had a chance—'

His words were swallowed by the importunate wail of the cattle-boat whistle. Reaching them through the rainy darkness, the sound was urgent and imperative. Flanagan again jerked his head in the direction of the river.

'There's not a blessed thing we can do here, boys. Besides, this is no concern of ours anyway.'

'We can't just leave him this way,' one said.

'It ain't our worry,' Flanagan almost shouted, now half-way off down the laneway. 'Come . . .'

14

He broke off. The door of the nearest hovel suddenly opened to emit a beam of light that fell brightly over the dead man and the three kneeling figures who suddenly lifted their faces. A slatternly woman stood there framed in the doorway, staring as though frozen. Then she emitted a shattering scream and slammed the door shut with a crash, howling blue murder from behind it.

'We didn't do it!' the young one said, was ready to say more when a powerful hand seized his elbow. He swung to stare up into Flanagan's strained face.

'For tarnal's sake, get movin'!' he pleaded. 'You can hear that boat – and there's not a blessed blind thing can be done here. And listen to that hollerin'. That female'll bring the law in jig time, and from what we've seen of how they feel about Westbounders, they might just swing the lot of us and start asking questions later.'

As though on cue, a man's voice sounded from somewhere close by.

'What in tarnation is goin' on out there for Pete's sake?'

'Murder!' came the woman's piercing voice from behind the door. 'Foul, dastardly murder right on a body's own doorstep. Three of the blackguards, mebbe four. Westbounders they are. Where's the sheriff when you need the pot-bellied varmint?'

Suddenly acutely aware of their own danger the three new friends traded one long look, turned to stare at Flanagan, then jumped to their feet and ran. The blacksmith was right, they realized. There was

15

nothing to gain by staying, unless they wanted to tempt a lynch mob. This was the West, not Virginia.

They were tramping up the gangplank of the battered old cattle boat by the time the law reached Fishbone Alley.

The party from the jailhouse approached the knot of people clustered about the dead man. The onlookers parted and Sheriff Buck Flory dropped to one knee alongside the corpse. There was no need to look for signs of life. Times like this the sheriff of Cairo was always calm and controlled. His deputies looked sick but he was efficiency itself as he searched the dead man's pockets in search of clues and identification.

'Robbery, I'd hazard,' he grunted, rising to his feet. 'Miner by the rig. Might have been carrying something valuable.' He filled his lungs to shout: 'Hey, Mrs Jacrosse! It's the sheriff. You can open your door now.'

The door opened a crack and a solitary fearful eye peered out. Then it was flung wide and the slattern emerged clutching a wine-bottle by the throat. She glared accusingly at the corpse, then the law.

'A murder right on a body's own stoop. What is this dirty town comin' to?'

'That's for me to find out,' growled the law. 'You see what happened?'

Flattered to find herself the focus of the attention, the woman made a grotesque attempt to primp her ratty hair.

'I heard all the screechin' and hollerin', and when

I took a belt to give me courage, I flung me door open and there they were – three of the butchers kneelin' around him, and him already starin' into the eye of the Saviour, all stiff and stark he was with that dirty great blade—'

'Did you recognize these men?' Flory demanded.

'They looked like Westbounders to me. You know? Fancy clothes and clean-shaved. Eastern dudes iffen you ask me. There was another feller in back of 'em who coulda been local.'

'Anything else?'

She frowned. 'Well . . . I guess the three was all kinda tall and kinda youngish . . .' She nodded. 'Yeah, that about sums 'em up, I guess.'

'Would you know them again if you saw them?'

'I can only hope and pray I'll never see any one of 'em again as long as I live.'

Flory frowned down at the man lying at his feet. He dealt with many crimes in his town but fortunately murder was rare. But he felt in no way sure that he might find the guilty parties in this case, considering the circumstances and the unreliability of the sole witness.

'Tote him round to the office and go get Judge Smith,' he instructed. 'Madam, seeing as you're our only witness you can come along and tell the judge what you just told me. All right, let's move.'

The sheriff had natural authority. Ready hands hefted the corpse and, with the knife still protruding from his chest, the victim was borne away.

'Right on me doorstep,' Mrs Jacrosse informed

those onlookers who'd arrived late. 'I could've been murdered in me bed. It's them Easterners o' course . . . uppity foreigners and riff-raff if you ask me . . .'

The rain came down in sheets again but nobody paid much attention. Out upon the big river, a laden cattle boat threshed its way against the rising flood. It would be the last trip that night. Whoever was not aboard had missed his last chance to join the train scheduled to leave at dawn for the Golden West.

CHAPTER 2

VENGEANCE IS MINE!

The sheriff sighed and slumped deeper into his chair. He supposed he should be grateful that folks were showing up to view the remains in the hope of making a positive identification, yet he suspected most were driven by ghoulish curiosity.

So he largely ignored what was going on about him and swung his swivel-chair to stare bleakly out into the morning street – his overcrowded morning street.

The midnight cattle boat had been the last to make it across to the western shore. The river was now running a-banker and the hundreds who'd arrived too late overnight were now wandering up and down the main stems like lost souls, worrying and wondering how long it might be before they would get to make the crossing.

The novelty of the Westbounders was rapidly wearing thin for Buck Flory yet they still fascinated to a degree.

Today he watched red-faced and muscular men from the Kentucky minefields chew smoked uncured tobacco and command the center of the muddy sidewalks as they tramped about, looking for someone to blame for the flooded river.

He glimpsed Pennsylvania-Dutch peasants, fair-headed, unsmiling, clean-scrubbed. There were families from Brooklyn, pale-faced and pock-marked, the men walking with a swagger cultivated upon stone streets, the women thin and shrunken yet still unable to conceal the hope in their faces.

Crackers, a religious group from Georgia with long rifles, stiff-necked folks in good clothes and smelling of scent, from Boston; hopefuls from Ohio and failures from the Carolinas – they all passed by in parade and the lawman wished them further as he'd seen it all before.

Then it happened. Half a block away he spotted a man who stood out from the crowd in such a singular way that he actually found himself leaning forward to get a better glimpse, when a hand tapped his shoulder.

'Shurf,' said the deputy. 'Mrs Robinson says to tell you it ain't her George.'

Flory stared at the man, then at the old woman shuffling out. He cussed.

'Goddamnit, man, she's eighty, her old man ran out on her forty years ago, and she still expects to find him?'

'Ah, she's a good old soul. Er, what was you just lookin' at, Sheriff?'

Flory stared out. There was no sign of that towering figure which had caught his eye. He heaved himself upright and made an impatient gesture.

'Clear them out. I'm convinced that that miner, or whatever he was, was a total stranger and we'll be lucky if we ever get to identify him. We've done enough, damnit. I'll just write up a report and . . .'

His voice trailed away and he stepped aside as the deputies ushered the last ghoulish viewers from the cell block where the dead man lay. He heaved a sigh of relief as the last man vanished, turned to his desk and was about to lower himself behind it when the sound of footsteps told him someone else had come in off the street.

'It's all over for today—' he snapped, turning, but broke off in mid sentence.

'You, sir, I take it, are the sheriff here?'

Buck Flory turned and stared.

In Cairo these days a man got to see just about every breed there was, yet this one was surely different. And taller. Flory estimated him at over six feet four, looked even taller as he was dressed head to toe in unrelieved black. His shoulders were broad, his middle lean, and he stood as straight as a Springfield rifle as he stared down upon Flory's five feet eight with a mixture of arrogance and annoyance.

Flory realized he was gaping, and that was uncharacteristic. He put on his most officious bulldog expression and waved at the door.

'Show's over,' he said gruffly.

'I beg your pardon, sir?'

The deep voice seemed to shake the office and the man made no move for the door. Instead he moved a deliberate step closer, forcing the lawman to back up a pace.

Flory reddened as he took a second look.

The man was a total stranger – you'd never forget anybody who looked like this. His head was large and he wore shoulder-length black hair, dusted with gray. The powerful face was dominated by piercing dark eyes burning beneath black brows that seemed to drill through the rotund lawman like augers.

Flory sat down suddenly and again set his jaw in familiar hard lines.

'Deputies! Show this fellow the gate and don't—'

'I'm still waiting,' the apparition cut in. 'For you to identify yourself, that is, sir. I'll ask again. Are you the sheriff or are you not?'

'He . . . he's Sheriff Flory, mister,' put in a pale-faced deputy. They were used to all kinds here, or at least had thought that to be the case up until now. 'Er . . . what do you want?'

'Doone,' the stranger stated, removing his flat-brimmed black hat and passing it to the deputy without looking at him. 'Preacher Ethan Doone, at your service.'

'You're a minister?' Flory asked, rising slowly despite himself. Then he began to recover his composure; he put on his familiar rifle-bore frown. 'Damnit if you don't look more like a damn pool-shark gambler to me, mister.'

Black eyes flared.

'Not "mister" – mister. "Preacher".'

'Baptist or Episcopalian?' retorted the law, determined not to be intimidated.

'I owe no allegiance to any regimented sects or corrupt churches,' came the reply. 'I am, as I said, a minister of the Lord. I preach, I combat the devil, I bring the Word. Does a man need to have a worthless diploma from some barren theological institute, or to wear his collar the wrong way about to do such work?'

It was at that point that the rugged sheriff's defiance began seriously to falter.

'Er, I guess not, parson.'

'Preacher. Now, sir, I arrived in your sin-ridden town just two hours earlier from the south to keep an appointment with my brother whom I have not seen in several years. I received a letter from him a week ago, stating that he would be in Cairo today, and identifying his lodgings. I find however that he hasn't been seen there since some time yesterday, which I find very strange. I have been searching all over but without luck, so I made the decision to visit here in the hope that you may be able to assist me in my search.'

Flory shook his head.

'There's hundreds of strangers passing through here every day, man . . . drifters, migrants, fortune-hunters—'

'My brother is none of those things, Sheriff. He is a prospector and a respectable citizen, a husky, hard-working man ten years my junior.'

'Uh-huh. So what does he look like?'

'He lacks some of my height, though a tall man still. He is thirty-six years of age, dark hair, brown skin from the outdoor life and the rough hands of a man who works hard. He regrettably displayed a tendency towards wildness at times, and is no stranger to the demon drink or to the hell-world of the gambling-dens either, I regret to say.'

'Anything else?' the sheriff said, a grim suspicion beginning to form in his mind. 'Any identifying marks or scars?'

Doone frowned.

'I have not seen my brother in some years and therefore do not know what ravages time may have wrought. But as a boy he lost part of one finger—'

'Little finger right hand?'

'Why, yes, I believe so. Then you have encountered him, sir?'

'Maybe you'd better accompany me in back, Preacher Doone.'

'I don't understand.'

'I have a feeling you will in a minute. I got something to show you.'

The body lay upon a bench covered by a canvas sheet in the second cell. Grim-faced, the lawman entered ahead of the visitor and pulled the sheet back to reveal the face. Doone gasped and every last vestige of color fled his face.

'Abel!' he gasped.

'This is your brother, Preacher?'

Doone dropped to his knees beside the bench and

took the dead man's hands in his own.

'My brother,' he whispered. 'My sole living relative – gone!'

'I'm right sorry, reverend—'

'Preacher.' Doone rose stiffly, seeming to loom even taller over the runty peace officer as he drew a deep breath into his chest. 'Tell me exactly how my brother died.'

Doone obliged. Doone heard him out in silence, then snapped his fingers.

'Kindly conduct me to the crime scene and the residence of this Mrs Jacrosse.'

'It's the rough side of town down by the docks and I've already told you what she—'

'I do not care to repeat myself, Sheriff.'

Buck Flory was a hard man who didn't bluff easily. Normally, that was. He was already convinced that this intimidating and impressive so-called man of the cloth seemed a far cry from normal.

'I'll get my hat,' was all he said, hating himself for folding while lauding himself for doing the wise thing.

By the time the two reached the docks area Doone had ceased sniffing audibly at the evidence of decay, drunkenness and immorality to be seen on every side. He fell totally silent as they eventually reached the grimy cul-de-sac and its semicircle of tumble-down shanties. He was staring down at the deep scuff-marks in the drying mud at his feet, the streaks of bloody crimson.

He raised his head as a door creaked open and a

rheumy eye peered out.

'What are you doin' back here, Buck Flory—' a shrewish voice began, but was cut off by the preacher.

'Mrs Jacrosse?' he guessed, going forward. 'Preacher Doone. Good lady, I am the bereaved brother of the young man who was most foully done to death here before your residence last night. Naturally I shall seek retribution for this atrocity but before I attempt to do so I must be certain of my facts. Might I come in?'

Flory fully expected her to tell him to go straight to hell. But the excitement of the murder backed up by this strangely impressive one's arrival was the biggest thing to happen to Muriel Jacrosse in a coon's age, and moments later the sheriff found himself cooling his heels on the stoop while the preacher and the lady conducted their business indoors.

It was a full twenty minutes before Doone emerged, a besotted Mrs Jacrosse trailing after him.

'Three Westbounders, you say, Muriel?' he reviewed, halting on the stoop after having elbowed Flory off it. 'Tall, well-dressed, in their twenties by your estimation ... and possibly a fourth man in their company?'

'Yes, Preacher Doone. But you must be rememberin' that with the poor light and me being so horrified and all, I only really saw one clear. He was kneeling by you poor dear brother and looking up at me; startled as sin he was.'

'Handsome, would you say?'

'For a dirty killer? I suppose he was. And like I say, the two flanking him were dressed alike, like stuck-up Easterners, you understand. The fourth geezer was only like a dim shape, but I could tell he was older, heavier and was dressed rough. Like plain everyday folks, not flash—'

'You're to be commended for your recollection, considering the impact this bloody assassination would have had on a woman of refinement and sensibility such as yourself, madam.'

Mrs Lacrosse flushed girlishly. She hadn't attracted a halfway decent compliment in years.

'Why, thank you, Preacher Doone. And I'll be praying tonight that you bring these evil persons to justice.'

'Muriel, if you could be as certain of riding to Heaven in a golden chariot as you can be of my vengeance, then you would be packing your bags in preparation right now.'

'Ooh, you do speak lovely . . . even if I'm not quite sure what you're saying, Preacher—'

'I am saying thanks from the bottom of my heart, dear lady.' So saying he lifted her hand, kissed it then turned away with a grunt to Buck Flory, who hated himself all over for the docile way he fell in behind.

'My brother had no gold or possessions when you took his body in, Sheriff?' Doone questioned as they cleared the cul-de-sac.

'Nothing,' Flory panted. 'But some witnesses claimed they saw him with a satchel just before he was jumped.'

Doone nodded. 'That would have have been his gold. So, he was butchered like a beast for a handful of worthless dust!'

'Well, a bag of gold wouldn't be exactly worth-less . . .' Doone broke off. 'Er, where are we going now?'

'The docks of course. Someone may have seen something there.'

'I questioned some of the hands who took the last barge over and back. They don't recollect seeing anything unusual.'

It was as if the lawman hadn't spoken. Ten minutes later found them at the river levee, staring out at the misting rain shrouding the grossly swollen river. Doone remained standing there a long time, just staring across at the almost invisible west bank. Somehow Doone found the man almost as intimidat-ing when silent as when talking.

Eventually Doone sighed and turned away. He indicated a rude cabin hard by the water's edge, with smoke coming from the rusty tin chimney.

'That where the ferry masters hole up?'

'Uh-huh. Guess you want to talk to them, huh?'

'As you failed to do, sir? Yes I certainly do. Lead the way.'

For a time it appeared that none of the hard-bitten characters who plied the river had seen anything unusual or of value on the night in question. Aggressive by nature and normally rough-tongued, they at first appeared subdued in Doone's presence, answering his queries soberly, but seemingly unrewardingly. As the two were about to quit the shack, a snore rose from a two-tiered bunk against the wall behind them.

'Cranky Bob,' offered a helmsman by way of explanation. 'He took the last boat across last night. Had a bit of a rough trip comin' back.'

'The last boat . . . ?' Doone's lower lip jutted. 'And what is he doing asleep in the middle of God's day?'

'Sleepin' off a drunk,' growled a man with the flattened features of a brawler. 'The river scares him when it's comin' up and he hits the bottle to keep his nerves steady, I guess.'

Doone strode to the bunk. He reached out and shook a shoulder roughly. There was a muffled grunt, followed by the emergence of a bleary, grizzled head. Cranky Bob stared uncomprehendingly at the strange face a moment, then swore foully.

Doone's big hands flashed out, swift as rattlesnakes. Seizing the man's shoulders, he wrenched him bodily clear of the bunk and dumped him on the floor with a thud. More curses. Doone grabbed his shirtfront and reefed the man into a standing position – no mean feat considering Cranky Bob weighed over 200 pounds.

The sheriff looked uneasy. Cranky Bob was no stranger to his cells. He could fight like a threshing machine, and often did when on the whiskey.

'Is this how you choose to spend your God-given time on this earth, you sodden piece of excrement?' the preacher demanded, giving him a bone-rattling shake. 'Drowning your senses in alcohol then compounding your baseness with profanity? Well, speak up, you poltroon. Is it?'

Cranky Bob regarded himself as a man of action. Fully awake and outraged by this time he let out a roar and aimed a kick at the preacher's groin.

It missed. But Doone's punch connected with a resounding crack. The man's eyes glassed and he would have fallen had not the other held him up.

'Now, sir, you conducted the last boat across the river before the flood closed it? Is that so?'

Cranky wasn't cranky any longer. He was terrified and thought he might have a busted jaw. He nodded, not yet able to get his voice working again.

'Did you see anything suspicious on that journey? A man was murdered last night and the men responsible took your boat. Three of them together, perhaps four. The three were young and respectable-looking, or so I'm told. Well, you sodden wreck?'

'Well . . . well, now I come to think of it I did see a bunch of fellers that kinda fit your description. And mebbe . . . just mebbe mind, one of 'em might have had bloodstains on the sleeve of his jacket as I recall.'

'Who were they? I want names?'

'We never get names. All we want is that they pay their passage—'

'No more? Nothing?'

The riverman shook his sorry head then crashed backwards into the wall behind the preacher's angry shove. He was slowly sliding to the floor as Doone strode from the shack with the law in his wake.

The rain was coming down hard but Doone

seemed oblivious to it as he stood glaring stonily across the Mississippi.

'They're over there,' he ground out. 'I have a picture of them in my mind. But where shall they be by the time the accursed waters go down?'

'Long gone, I'd hazard,' Flory replied. 'But you can rely on me to notify the authorities over there just as soon as I'm able, although I wouldn't get my hopes up if I was you.

'You see, preacher, the ferrymen calculate it'll most likely be five days to a week before anyone can cross. In that time those Westbounders and the wagons will be to hell and gone. The Company has sent any number of trains out there over the past couple years and those wagon masters have mapped out all-weather tracking clear to the Cimarron. Take my word for it, those teamsters hustle their Conestogas along from daylight to dark, fair weather or foul. The truth of it is, that train and the killers could be clear to Texas by the time the law could—'

'You don't have to worry about the law pursuing those men, Sheriff.'

'I don't?'

The tall figure turned slowly. 'No, that shall be my sacred duty.'

'You, Preacher? But you're a man of the cloth. Those killers could be professionals even if they mightn't look it. And if you did get to catch up with them I reckon that in view of the way they did your brother they sure wouldn't hesitate in sending you to join him. No, take my advice. This is a job for the bounty hunters, or a US marshal, not a preacher-man.'

'I am a man first, a servant of the Lord second, lawman,' Doone intoned in his pulpit voice. 'My beloved brother, the only blood kin I had in all this benighted world has been foully done to death. As a man – not a man of the cloth – it is my sacred bounden duty to avenge him.'

'But—'

'You think that it is simply hatred or lust for vengeance that burns within in my breast? You fool! Of course I grieve for my brother. Who would not? But he was a mortal man and every one of us knows that death, the inevitable end, will surely come to us all. As for the gold? Worthless dust. But what I can never forgive is the fact that my brother intimated to me in his most recent letters that he was at last prepared to surrender his sinful ways and follow in the steps of his divine master. Do you comprehend? Right here, in your stinking bordello of a slum town, he intended to embrace the Cross!'

Tough Flory was almost intimidated. But mostly he was just puzzled.

'So?' he said, regretting the word almost before it was out of his mouth.

Hands of extraordinary power seized his shirtfront and reefed him to his feet. Blazing eyes were but inches from his own.

'He who steals my gold steals trash. He who takes the life of another may be forgiven if he repents. But the crime that was committed here can only be expiated by the blood of those responsible. Why? you might ask in your ignorance. Because those who took my brother's life robbed him of the salvation of his immortal soul, and not even the Divine Lord could find it in his heart to forgive that!'

Moments later a dazed Buck Flory found himself alone. He realized he needed a stiff drink.

CHAPTER 3

IN THE NAME
OF THE FATHER

'Here it is, Ash.'

Ash Carmody, editor of Wagontown's bi-weekly, the *Western Globe*, took the mock-up of the paper from his type-slinger and studied it. He only scanned the front page for, in this particular edition, that was the only page that really counted. With an expert eye he detected one inverted letter. He drew it to Hanrohan's attention.

'Fix it then print,' he said.

When Hanrohan failed to respond immediately, Carmody glanced up from his desk. 'That's today and not next week, Dobie.' He indicated the clock above the door. 'It's near four now. If we don't get moving we won't have it out come five-thirty.'

The typesetter tugged at his sad gray mustaches

with fingers so blackened by printer's ink they would never be really clean again.

'This here is pretty strong meat, Ash,' he muttered. He was a Georgian with a banjo drawl.

Carmody frowned. Tall, well-made and still on the right side of thirty, he was not yet stooped from bending over galleys, still boasted a flat middle not yet thickened from his wife's excellent cooking. He was puzzled by Hanrohan's remarks. The man seldom commented beyond printing technicalities and left the editorial policy to him, which was as it should be.

'It's got to be strong or it won't have the punch, Dobie.'

'There's such a thing as too much punch, I guess.'

'You reckon this has got too much?'

'No, siree. You're just calling a spade a spade, I guess.'

'Then why the reservations?'

'Honest John Marchant was one powerful aggravated saloonman when you went after him in the *Globe* last month, if you remember, Ash. I'm just anticipating how he might react when he reads this editorial on top of that, is all.'

'It's the old story about making an omelette, I guess, Dobie. You can't make one unless you crack a few eggs.'

Hanrohan shrugged thin shoulders and pushed his way through the gate in the railing that divided the office from the printing-shop.

'Well, so long as eggs are the only things that get cracked, I guess it's all right.'

Carmody watched the type-slinger thrust his head and hands into the black bowels of the Wiesburger, still frowning and still plainly ill at ease.

He picked up the copy of the paper and re-read his editorial carefully once again. Was it too strongly worded? Maybe so. But what else would convince a blatant crook, con-man and exploiter like Honest John Marchant that Wagontown was not his to plunder, and with nobody prepared to raise a single objection?

He was still scanning the paper, with the Weisburger rattling and rolling out the newspapers in the background, when the door leading to the living-quarters opened and Ruth came through. As was her habit in the late afternoons, she had changed her dress and looked fresh and sparkling. He put the paper aside and leaned back with a smile.

'You generally catch me loafing,' he said.

She sat down in the chair reserved for visitors.

'When I heard the machine start up I knew you were almost through.' She smiled brightly. 'You see? I'm beginning to learn the newspaper business already – after only three months married. Aren't I smart?'

He nodded. 'And beautiful.'

It had been a whirlwind romance that had begun a year after his arrival in town. Several months later he'd taken the big step and set up his own newspaper in Kansas. It made him feel good to reflect that both his business and his marriage appeared to be prospering.

They chatted for several minutes before Ruth, glancing around, frowned faintly.

'What's wrong with Dobie? He didn't greet me when I came in. Has he got his heartburn again?'

'Not this time. He just reckons the editorial is too strong, is all.'

'Oh, that's the one about Marchant which you stayed up half the night to get right, isn't it?'

He handed her the paper. 'See what you think.'

She read the headline aloud.

'Gambler Fleeces Honest Citizens!' She looked up sharply. 'Honey, that is rather bold, isn't it?'

'Read the rest.'

She scanned the article halfway, then began reading aloud:

'It's been brought to the notice of this newspaper that a prospector, Charlie Savage by name, lost almost a thousand dollars recently playing roulette at Marchant's establishment, in the process making eleven consecutive losing wagers. The odds against this happening on an honest wheel must be immense, which poses the question. Is the wheel at the Lucky Dice an honest one?'

They discussed the matter for some time. He took note of her comments but it didn't change his mind. He believed a newspaper had a responsibility to make social comment as well as present the news. He was a stubborn man and knew it, and in this case was strongly disinclined to back down.

'I'm not saying there's anything wrong with the piece, Ash. It's just the repercussions I worry about. Marchant is a rather ruthless man, I suspect. He certainly has that reputation. I just wonder what would happen to our business were he to try to undermine us if he took exception to a piece like this. I saw how hard you worked and saved to get the paper going after coming all the way from Virginia. I'd hate to see you perhaps lose it on a simple point of morality.'

His face tightened.

'I hope I'm a newspaperman first and a business-man second, honey. I mean to keep on after Marchant until he either mends his ways or closes down.'

'Just like Rand Malleroy?'

'Exactly like Rand.'

'You realize some people will say what they've said before? That you show favoritism to Rand and his saloon.'

He shrugged. The charge wasn't new. Rand Malleroy, just a year older than himself, had been with him and Wes Shelby on the big train from Cairo a year ago. The three had shared some good times, and one really bad experience. It had been a casual friendship which seemed to have dissolved when, for different reasons, each of them had chosen to branch off to different destinations upon reaching the real West.

Shelby had been the only one to choose Wagontown

originally, and was installed as sheriff by the time a failed venture farther west brought Malleroy to the town, eventually to take over the Two Bits saloon.

Two months later Carmody showed up with his then fiancée after hearing of a newspaper up for grabs. He'd stayed on, all three had made different lives and new friends but occasionally they all got together again, mainly to relive the epic journey, then went on about their separate lives.

Favoritism was not the reason Ash rarely attacked Malleroy in the *Western Globe*. It was because he knew him to be an honest man who ran straight games. He said as much now. Ruth appeared to understand.

'You don't tell me how to cook so I guess I should-n't tell you how to run a newspaper.' She smiled, rising to go. 'But I do worry for your safety. I've heard Marchant has a record of some kind.'

He smiled up at her. 'You shouldn't believe all you read in the newspapers.'

'All right, all right.' She laughed. Then, turning at the sound of the door to the street, she added: 'And speaking of whom, I'll leave you old Virginians to sit around and gossip, as you love to do. Hi, Wes!' she called and disappeared as the sheriff of Wagontown came in, taking off his hat.

Wes Shelby was a man of roughly Carmody's age and height, but fairer of complexion and heavier of physique. His face was square-jawed, tanned and truculent, in a clear-eyed, boyish kind of way. He was dressed in plain rig and wore a five-pointed star on his calfskin vest.

'Long time no see, Wes,' Carmody greeted as he went to the pot-belly to pour coffee into tin pannikins.

When he returned to the desk the sheriff was scanning the front page of the *Western Globe*. He looked up sharply and Carmody shook a warning finger.

'No lectures. Ruth's already taken me to task about the Marchant piece.'

Shelby sipped his coffee and nodded appreciatively.

'Hell, I like it, Ash. That stuff about Charlie Savage losing all that money is the truth. I reckon you'd know that Charlie lives out in the hills like a gopher most of the year, panning for gold. You can imagine how long it would take him to make a thousand, but it only took Marchant one night to relieve him of it.'

'Ruth frets that he might start something when he sees the paper.'

'I'll be around to see he doesn't.'

Carmody grinned. Wes Shelby had developed into a tough loner who'd fitted into the lawman's job more quickly and more comfortably than he'd succeeded here at the *Globe*. Wagontown was a broad-shouldered, two-fisted kind of town of the wide plains which had had more than its share of lawlessness before the original sheriff retired after being wounded in a gunfight, leaving the chair empty for Shelby to fill.

Times like this it seemed far more than eighteen months ago since he, Shelby and Rand Malleroy had met and parded up on the westbound wagon train.

Seemed they'd been more like boys than men then. But if the West did nothing else for a man it assured he matured fast.

They took their coffee out onto the front gallery and watched their adopted town in the afternoon. Shelby indicated a bearded man driving slowly by in a wagon with cut-under front gear, man and rig looking like they'd seen many a hard mile together.

'Westbounder,' said the sheriff. 'Came the same route as we did, so he tells me. Crossed at Cairo.'

The two traded glances. Cairo seemed a long way in the past even though it was only a year; so much had happened since. But they would never forget the river town, or what had happened there. Ash Carmody believed the killing they'd come across there that night had both matured and hardened them for what lay ahead for them in the 'real' West.

'Guess Cairo'd still be much the same, huh?' he commented.

'A little quieter, so I gather.'

'Wonder if they ever caught the bastard killed that prospector?'

'I asked him about that but he didn't know anything. I reckon, when you look back, Cairo was the sort of place where it might be easy enough to get yourself killed.'

They were silent with their memories for a time before until the Misses Hunter came swishing by. Two of the town's sterling pillars of morality, and determined spinsters, the sisters closed in looking severe and grim. They believed that the *Globe* ran far too many unsavory articles on crime and corruption, and considered Sheriff Shelby as much too ready to employ a billy-club or even a Colt .45 in the execution of his duty.

The good ladies sniffed as they sailed by.

'You know, if I could sign Priscilla and Deborah up as deputies, Ash, I believe this place could become as decent and law-abiding as Cosgrove, Virginia in jig time.'

The newsman chuckled. 'Mebbe it will be that way in time, Wes. It sure is something good to aim at.'

'No reason why it shouldn't, I hope. Well, see you, Ash. Time for my rounds.' Shelby smiled. 'We'll have to get together for a drink some night. It's been months.' He winked. 'Want me to take a paper along to the Lucky Dice for Marchant?'

'I reckon he'll get his hands on a copy soon enough.'

Carmody remained on the gallery long after the sheriff had gone. It was good to relax and take the evening air and smell the honeysuckle after a long day cooped up in the office.

Dobie eventually called out to report that the edition was completed. The typesetter had apparently forgotten about his reservations concerning the Marchant article and invited his boss to join him at the Two Bits saloon, owned and operated by Rand Malleroy, the third member of the party which had come to Wagontown via the fateful Mississippi crossing.

It developed into a great evening, and strolling

homewards in the moonlight Ash Carmody felt very much at peace, a man of his place and time. Yet for some reason before he reached home he found himself halting and looking around as though he'd either heard or sensed something in the night which seemed to unsettle him, the kind of feeling he imagined a man might get in a dream when he felt someone walk over his grave.

He shook himself and forced a grin. This was so uncharacteristic of himself that he was at once both surprised and annoyed. He knew it wasn't Marchant and his editorial that was playing on his mind; he'd encountered the big man earlier and although far from friendly, the Lucky Dice boss appeared to be shouldering the attack by the paper in his customary assured manner.

What then?

He stood there until the sensation faded, then walked on. He was glad to find that Ruth had waited up for him. He didn't tell his wife or anybody else that for some loco reason he scarcely closed his eyes that night.

Could be he needed a vacation.

'Lust!' boomed the man in black, 'is the curse of the West!'

That caused them to sit up and take notice. The good citizens of frontier Gullytown were fairly inured against sermons on such subjects as pride, covetousness, envy, anger and sloth which aroused little excitement. But lust? That was a totally different kettle of fish. Lust was a topic any God-fearing citizen could really sink his teeth into on a bright Sunday morning.

'Sins of the flesh,' continued the man of God, 'are the greatest corruptor of moral fibre and cause of more heartache and misery than any other. . . .' Here he paused for dramatic effect and all leaned forward eagerly to hear what came next. 'Any other, that is, but the foul and unforgivable sin and crime of murder!'

The congregation of the Church of the Holy Sepulchre slumped back in disappointment. Where had murder crept in? Sure, they were all against it; who wouldn't be? But if they had their druthers they would rather sit through a dozen steamy sermons on the topic of carnality than a single one dedicated to murder.

But their disappointment wasn't due to last long, as they quickly discovered. For when Preacher Doone, towering above them from the boxwood pulpit of the clapboard-and-panel house of worship, launched into the subject of murder most foul, even the slowest amongst them soon realized this was developing into something very different from the sort of hair-raising sermons that had seen Doone pack out their hitherto neglected place of worship over the past eventful week.

Listening to the compelling tirade, people felt he was dealing with something that moved him far more deeply on a personal level than anything they'd heard from him thus far.

He described in grisly detail the brutal killing of a prospector on the streets of Cairo, Kentucky, then abruptly revealed that this was a true story and that the man in question had been his brother and only living relative. He added that he had not arrived at Gullytown by chance, but by design.

'I believe that some of you, my dear brothers and sisters,' he said emotionally, 'came west via Cairo, Kentucky, more than a year past now. That is what brought me to your town, this knowledge. You see, for a year and more, while bringing the word west, I have been patiently and prayerfully seeking someone, anyone, who may have seen or heard anything of the merciless footpads who put my brother in the earth and broke my heart. So therefore, tonight, I want you to do two things for me. One, contribute generously when Brother Kelp and the sisters bring around the plate – for my quest must continue and I have no sustenance but that which you provide. And secondly, and more important, should any of you have any information, any clue to the identity or destinations of those three slaughtermen of the devil whom I've described to you, please don't be afraid to come forward and thus earn my everlasting gratitude and a ticket to Paradise.'

The collection proved a record for the Gullytown church, for Preacher Doone was the most eloquent man of God they'd ever seen.

But the result of the second request was bitterly disappointing. The preacher waited an hour in the vestry after the service was over but the only citizen who came forward was one of the many enemies he'd already made in his short time here. This one was no worshipper, and arrived with a pair of hard-faced deputy sheriffs and an air of venomous self-satisfaction.

The town commissioner didn't believe either in God or 'Bible-bashers' who landed uninvited in his bailiwick, then proceeded to act like they were above the law.

It turned out that the pompous official of Gullytown County had been both busy and successful on some private business of his own over the forty-eight hours, ever since the pair had last clashed over an incident in which Doone had broken a citizen's arm during a saloon brawl.

'So tell me, how did the meeting go tonight, Preacher?'

He was a mean-eyed man with a drooping black mustache who regarded himself as the most important figure in town. As such, it had been inevitable that the two would lock horns. The preacher's mission assured that.

During the past year, armed with passenger manifests from the Cairo wagon train, Doone had visited countless cities, towns and simply wide places in the road in his hunt for his brother's killers.

It was his high-handed nature to power his way through, to tread on toes and bruise vanities. This had been the case with the commissioner whom he had humiliated publicly on two occasions when temper and raging impatience got the better of him.

46

But tonight the townsman's self-assurance had plainly returned. He both spoke and looked like a winner as his mustache lifted to a mocking grin.

'Milk the suckers again, did you – holy man?'

Doone's eyes were unfathomable pools of blackness. During the service he'd appeared as an inspired bringer of the Word, with his harsh and menacing side peeping through but briefly. But at this moment, with his flock gone and facing an enemy who'd even brought his own tin star security along with him tonight, he appeared, in knee-length black coat and with arms folded across his broad chest, exactly like the sort whom any one smart person would naturally avoid, if given the option.

'You have a point?'

'Why I do believe I do have a point about – shall we say – Cow Creek, Nebraska?'

Doone didn't respond. His visitor's smirk deepened offensively.

'Ahh, I see that strikes home,' he said with relish. 'You see – Preacher – you have raised so much dust here in my town and offended so many citizens with your high-and-mighty ways, that I just knew you couldn't be any kind of cleanskin. So I used my power and position to contact a wide spectrum of certain agencies and law enforcement bodies at various major centers between Colorado and the Mississippi regarding a gentleman who goes by the title of a preacher – yet who acts and looks more like some kind of fake or hellion.' A pause. 'And what did I discover? Or perhaps you would rather tell me?'

Doone folded his arms and locked his jaws. His brooding stare was a threat which the official chose to disregard as he nodded to the two deputies.

'That, gentlemen, is the look of a liar, a charlatan and a gunman! Or, would you care to deny, sir, that in the town of Cow Creek, Nebraska, in May last, you became engaged in an argument with a man you had been harrying regarding his suspected involvement in the murder of some kinsman of yours, and that in the ensuing gunplay you pumped three bullets into his heart?'

The deputies were stunned. Yet the preacher seemed remarkably calm.

'Self-defense,' he stated flatly. 'Your information would have also told you that a dozen witnesses who appeared at the hearing testified to the fact that it was a fair fight.' His eyes glittered. 'As it would be were you, sir, so moved to challenge me in my role as a missioner of the Lord either with your accusations . . . or perhaps with your guns . . . ?'

The commissioner paled and backed up a step.

'You . . . you heard that, gentlemen. He just threatened my life. Me! The town commissioner! I warned you he was outlaw scum, didn't I? Well, do your duty. Arrest him and my good friend the judge will see to it that he is dealt with under the full severity of the law. . . .'

He broke off suddenly. Slowly and deliberately, big-grown hands nimble, Doone unbuttoned the fitted long coat. He brushed the panels back and the three gaped at the gunrig buckled across flat hips.

The cartridge belt gleamed and the low-slung holster was thonged to the right thigh, gunslinger style. They saw that the weapon it held was a single action Colt .45.

'I am a man on a mission from God. I come to your stinking sin-ridden pest-hole of a town, not driven by vengeance as you imply, but in the name of the Father. My mission will be completed in blood whether it takes ten years or is fulfilled this night. I will kill those guilty of that unforgivable sin. I will also not hesitate to bury any stinking, lice-ridden dog, wolf, petty official or narrow-gutted peace officer who would delay me one moment in my holy task. On that understanding, either use those weapons or, if you don't have the stones for it, as I strongly suspect, get out of this holy place and go hide yourselves. For I am not through here, and if I meet any of you again, or any who might support you, no matter what number, I'll put you all in your lousy stinking graves, so help me God!'

The seconds hammered and the sound of the clock on the wall was a drumbeat. A deputy with a tough reputation coughed with dreadful dryness and stole a glance at the commissioner who had gone gray around the gills.

It was eerie, but the three men suddenly felt that they were in the presence of death, or at least the very real threat of it.

Eventually the lawmen moved crabwise for the doors. The commissioner hadn't expected this. Color flooding back to his face, he started in cussing them. But Doone's voice drowned him out.

'Sensible,' he said to the pair. Then his voice cracked like a whip. 'Now, get out!'

To their shame, the deputies jostled one another in their haste to get through the door. For a moment it seemed the commissioner felt rooted to the spot. Then he too made a break for it, only to be halted by the voice.

'Freeze, you son of a bitch!'

He froze, and Doone took two long strides to loom over him.

'You would impede God's work!' he whispered. 'You would dare?'

The terrified man opened his mouth to speak and a savage blow slammed it shut. He was falling when Doone grabbed his shirtfront with his left hand and used the right to deliver five brutal blows to head and body, each successive one heavier than the last.

He let the unconscious body fall to the floor and kicked it so hard it rolled fully over twice.

They were still fighting to bring the unconscious county commissioner around at the two-bed hospital an hour later when they heard the sounds of two horses loping off down main street, to fade slowly off into the night.

The preacher had never really believed his killers would be found here in Colorado Territory. When he halted to spell his horse two hours later on a hilltop, he grunted at his odd-looking companion as he leaned against his blowing horse and stared back the way they'd come.

'Another failure, Mr Kelp. How many hamlets, cities, farming communities, mining hells and shanty towns is that we've put behind us now?'

The little man blinked owlishly.

'Not like you to give in to negative thoughts, Preacher.'

'I had hopes for Gullytown . . . for some reason or another . . .'

'Might I make a suggestion, sir?'

This was a novelty. Mostly his acolyte simply followed orders and waited upon him hand and foot. Doone grunted assent and Kelp scratched his nose.

'Well, it seems to me, since I joined your crusade, that you always seem to holding back when you come to a place and start looking for your brother's killers. Sure, you work day and night watching folks, questioning them, looking for men that might match up to what those Westbounders might look like. But surely you'd stand a better chance of flushing them out if you were to – say – put out posters with descriptions of them you're after, and why. Or more simply, just get up on your hind-legs and make the sort of speech you made last night just as we were leaving. Do that at the start, and you never know who might come forward with information. . . .'

He paused. 'You're shaking your head, Preacher. . . .'

'Don't you think I'd do exactly that if I believed for a moment that it might harvest results?' Doone rarely appeared weary. He looked and sounded that way now.

'So why don't you—?'

'You just don't understand, Mr Kelp. With the precious little I have to go on, the killer or killers could be almost anybody. I mean . . . suspects tallish, possibly young, possibly – I say possibly – friends or travelling together.'

He spread his hands.

'Nearly everybody who comes West is young and reckless – they'd have to be to take the risks of Indians, cholera, smallpox and bloody-handed outlaws. And at least six out of every ten Westbounders are male. Add that to the fact that the crime took place more than a year ago now, giving those wagoners time to scatter to the four winds, and you could rightly rate my prospects as somewhere between slim and non-existent. So?'

'Er, so – Preacher?'

'So, all those factors considered, if I should blunder into a town and announce who I was hunting with almost no chance of identifying them on sight, I would be tipping my hand. And if by luck I were to act that way in a town harboring the guilty, they would have all the time and freedom in the world to simply pick up and vanish, probably for ever this time. Now perhaps you understand why I have to work slowly and secretly . . . searching for some link with the past, some vague hint that the realtor, blacksmith or even town mayor might have been in Cairo on that train, that night . . . in that evil slum. . . .'

The way Leander Kelp screwed up his face in fierce concentration indicated that he was at least

52

trying very hard to understand.

'But ... but you did tell why we'd come to Gullytown last night, Preacher.'

'I had nothing to lose by then. Either the guilty had never come near Gullytown, or if they had, I'd have scared them out by then. That appeal was the last shot in my locker. I hoped someone might know something, recall something ... but nothing, as you saw.'

'Don't give up, Preacher Doone.'

Doone actually half-smiled, realizing belatedly that he did feel vaguely more positive for having spoken of his ongoing problems and disappointments; he showed a glimmer of his normal energy and deci-siveness as he straightened. He drew a folded docu-ment from an inside pocket and scanned it by the light of a cold, white moon.

It was the inventory of a wagon train's passenger manifest, in this specific case a train that had made its way from West Virginia, across north Tennessee then up through Kentucky on its circuitous way west-ward one year and a half earlier.

Many of the names on the list had been crossed out by a grease pencil, each marking indicating the towns, cities, outposts, isolated spreads, farms and suchlike that he'd visited without success in his quest.

Deliberately now, he dragged his pencil through the name, Gullytown. Next on the manifest was yet another unfamiliar name, Wagontown.

He grunted again to his trail partner and they travelled on several miles before swinging off on a trail that switchbacked eastwards. Around noon next day they recrossed the border into Kansas.

CHAPTER 4

WAGONTOWN NIGHTS

The atmosphere was relaxed at the Two Bits saloon, so owner Rand Malleroy noted with approval as he emerged from his office to stand with his fingers in the slash pockets of his bed-of-flowers waistcoat and surveyed the crowd.

He paused to take it in. A good house tonight. His new singer was continuing to draw the paying customers. Then he sighted two special customers standing at the quieter end of his long mahogany bar. His eyes widened in surprise and immediately he headed their way, threading a path through the drinkers.

He paused to draw a packet of thin cigars from his pocket. He lighted the smoke one-handed with a pocket-flint and slipped it back into his jacket pocket. A strongly built man with good shoulders, the boss of Wagontown's second biggest watering-hole was always pleased to see friends from Virginia who'd made the great journey with him.

Sheriff and newsman greeted him warmly.

'About time,' grinned Carmody. 'It must be months since we downed one together.'

'We'll have to do it more often,' Shelby said. The others nodded yet doubted that that would happen. Change and responsibility altered things, as they'd discovered. They rarely got together these days due to work, pressure and circumstances. Even so, the mood was good as Shelby and Carmody offered to buy a round. But Malleroy shook his head.

'This is an occasion, strangers.' He smiled. 'Drinks are on me tonight.'

'Good crowd, Rand,' Sheriff Shelby remarked when they had fresh shots. He winked. 'Better be careful if your new singer draws too many paying customers away from the Lucky Dice.'

'John Marchant doesn't scare me any,' Malleroy insisted confidently. He lifted his glass and nodded. '*Salud.*'

They drank. Looking around and remembering old times, they glimpsed many a familiar face from the wagon train. Wagontown was a big bustling center situated on a verdant plain. It had industry, commerce and beef cattle and, being situated on the regular stage route, was predicted to have a big future. These and other reasons explained why so many of the Westbounders from the Cairo train had gravitated here after failing or being disappointed elsewhere.

As Carmody, Shelby and Malleroy had done, most

of the immigrants seemed to have settled in well, with only a small percentage either in regular trouble or actually down on their uppers.

In general the newcomers had been warmly welcomed by the citizens. But there was always an exception to any rule, and here the disapproving faction was led by Honest John Marchant. Regarded as Wagontown's richest and most powerful citizen, the big man was in the habit of frequently banning 'wagon-trainers' from his establishment on the grounds that they were 'shiftless, city rabble' or 'Johnny-come-latelies.' It was suspected his real reasons were far more complex than that. It was well known he didn't like Indians, black people, Mexicans, the poor, the successful or folks who voted Democrat. What he really liked was money and power, and was acquiring plenty of both.

'It just could be that Honest John's softening up some, you know,' Ash ventured. 'I mean, I expected a bad reaction from him after I ran that editorial on him last week. But even though he acted sore it seems he just let it go. That worries me a little because it's so out of character for our Mr Big.'

The boss of the Lucky Dice was a prime topic of interest around Wagontown in every quarter. The three were still airing their views on the man's latest business venture when a man came through the batwings and stood a moment, holding the louvred doors apart.

Not tall, but gaunt as a crab-apple-tree with buck teeth and steel-rimmed spectacles, the stranger was attired all in funeral black, a high celluloid collar and shiny black button-up boots. A high black topper perched squarely atop his knobby head. From behind the spectacles, little pale eyes as mean as a robber's dog's roamed the room and his nostrils were observed to twitch at whatever stink it was he detected about Rand Malleroy's wide-open Saturday-night saloon.

It was so seldom that the trio at the bar found themselves together these days that they were in a relaxed and even light-hearted mood. They saw the strange newcomer as a welcome diversion.

'I'll tell you something, Rand,' said Shelby, grinning. 'If Suzie is drawing your new clients these days, then she's sure pulling some odd ones. This one's new, isn't he?'

'Never saw him before,' Malleroy replied. 'You, Ash?'

'Nope. I know I'd remember him.' He frowned. 'He's not one of the crackers, is he?'

The so-called Crackers – recent arrivals from Georgia – were a strange clan of fundamentalist hill-folk who were currently making an impression on Wagontown, and not always a favorable one. Tonight's latest arrival certainly seemed strange-looking enough to fit in with the newcomers yet his sober attire was about as different from the Kentuckians' rough corn-patch calico and floppy-brimmed gray hats as you could get.

'Why's he holding the doors open?' Malleroy murmured curiously, as others also grew aware of the gaunt-faced stranger. 'He . . .'

He broke off as the man for whom the runt was waiting, brushed past him and strode into the light.

The noise-level dropped sharply and every head turned.

If the first stranger was unimpressive, the second occupied the opposite end of the spectrum. Standing there with feet planted wide and head flung back imperiously, he was tall, gaunt-faced and fiery-eyed and totally arresting. He wore severe black broad-cloth and from beneath his flat-brimmed hat, gray-streaked dark hair hung to his shoulders.

He conveyed the clear, instant impression that virtually everything that met his gaze deeply offended him on a personal level.

'One of those travelling sin-busters, do you figure?' Malleroy speculated.

'Looks pretty proddy if you ask me,' was the sheriff's reaction.

'Who's he staring at over by the bar?' Carmody wondered aloud.

The three sipped their drinks and continued to watch as the newcomer's attention appeared to focus upon a particular drinker at one of the tables.

The totally unaware customer was Willy Russell, part-time water-diviner and a most-of-the-time drunk. Lost in the oblivious world of the boozer's Shangri La, Willy was a fat little man with no hair on his head and no hint of awareness of the newcomer's burning-eyed interest. Until he glanced up to see the man standing over him, drilling him with a burning stare.

Willy blinked and hiccuped. Then he shook his head to clear his vision, but the towering figure remained.

'You, sir, are drunk!'

Again Willy Russell appeared puzzled, unsure whether he was being complimented or insulted.

'Miserably, soddenly, sinfully drunk!' the voice boomed, placing the matter beyond any doubt. By this almost everybody was watching and speculating on who the stranger might be and what he was about. They thought he looked unusual but hardly crazy.

'Lookit!' a drinker said. 'What's he doin' now?'

A big hand reached out and plucked the near-full glass from Willy's hand. Deliberately holding it clear of the table, the tall stranger emptied the contents onto the floor.

A shocked silence fell. Few things were held more sacred at the Two Bits than a man's liquor. A growing mutter of disapproval was rising as Willy leaned forward to stare blankly at the vast wet stain upon the floor. At an adjoining table, a thick-knuckled teamster hauled himself to his feet, bristling.

'Willy's a pard of mine,' he barked at the stranger. 'What the hell did you do that fer?'

As if awaiting exactly that query to be voiced, the fierce-faced stranger drew himself up and spoke loud enough for the entire room to hear.

'I am Preacher Ethan Doone, servant of the Lord and despiser of the demon rum!'

'Gawd strewth! Another stinking, white-blooded

holy Joe!' the teamster retorted, mouthing the words thickly.

Doone was upon the man in an instant. To his credit, the teamster managed to get one power-packed punch away but it failed to connect. The newcomer swayed easily out of reach then came back in behind a short driving right hand that exploded against a stubbled jaw with a crack like a blacksnake whip. As meaty legs buckled beneath him, the teamster took a second chopping blow to the back of the neck. He crashed into the floor, face first.

The saloon exploded.

Quitting his position against the wall nearby, Malleroy's case-keeper stepped forward, jaw set hard, sawn-off at the ready.

Malleroy motioned the man back.

But Doone had caught the threatening move from the corner of his eye. He swung lightning-fast to face the guard, deliberately fanning his coat panel back to reveal the silent challenge of holstered Colt .45 and a belt glinting with bronzed cartridge rims.

'I advise you to discard that back-shooter's weapon or use it, citizen!' he warned.

The guard swung uncertainly to glance at his boss. Ash Carmody spoke quietly.

'You'd best break this up before it gets out of hand, Rand. This stranger looks like serious trouble.'

'Just what I was thinking,' Malleroy said, stepping forward.

Without taking his eyes from the shotgun guard, Doone said evenly:

'Whoever you are, halt right there or you may be sorry.'

Malleroy paused. 'I'm Rand Malleroy, owner of the Two Bits. What the devil do you mean, busting in on a peaceful night and creating a ruckus?'

'This minion of yours made a threatening move with a firearm, sir. I'm still waiting to see if he intends backing it up.'

In the silence, Carmody glanced at Shelby.

'What do you reckon, Wes?'

'Rand's pretty capable in this sort of situation. With the words, I mean. If I horn in this madman might go off half-cocked.'

'You reckon he's mad?'

'Well, half-cracked leastways.'

'Take it easy, will you?' Malleroy was saying to the newcomer now, his voice conciliatory. 'My man's just doing the job I pay him for. Tell you what, let's forget the whole thing and let me buy you a drink, mister.'

'That's Preacher to you, sir,' Doone retorted. Yet he straightened, covered his gun with his coat and deliberately turning his back on the case-keeper, fixed a hard eye on Malleroy. 'No, you shan't be foisting any of your wicked spirits upon me, sir. And I note that both you and this yellow felon with the shotgun seem cut from the same cloth. By your manner and actions you demonstrate that you believe any man who is not too proud to go down upon his knees and pray, is a womanized creature . . . less than a man. Yet when that man calls your bluff, your cowardly spirits are exposed for all to see.' He

62

paused deliberately. 'Cowards. Do you not hear my words, corruptor of the weak?'

This was strong meat. Again Shelby started forward, but once more Carmody intervened.

'It's not worth it, Wes,' he said. 'Rand won't let him bait him. Let it ride, at least until we find out some more about this bird. Remember? You always say a lawman's job is to prevent fights, not help start them.'

Wesley stared at him for a long moment, then shrugged.

'You're right, Ash. Anyway, by the look of things our reverend – if that's what he is – seems to be cooling off now.'

Such did appear to be the case as the newcomer flicked his coat panel forward again to conceal the incongruous Colt.

'Well, if everybody is too pure yellow to stand up for your venal way of life . . .' He let that hang for a long moment in the obvious hope that someone might take offense. None did. He snorted and returned his focus to Malleroy. 'So, you are the proprietor of this hell-hole, sir?'

'I own the Two Bits. It's no hell-hole, and I like to keep it free of the kind of trouble you almost succeeded in kicking up.'

Doone looked at his top-hatted sidekick, then at the sea of attentive faces.

'Then I'm afraid that in the last respect you are due to be disappointed.'

'Howcome?'

'I did not come to your town or your establishment to create trouble. I arrived here with my acolyte, Mr Leander Kelp, just this afternoon at the end of a long journey, with the sole intention of saving souls, which I shall certainly do. You see, sir, on my way here I was overcome by a powerful feeling that I would find myself needed here, needed badly in truth.'

He arched black brows.

'That feeling is overpoweringly stronger right at this very moment. It seems I can scent the stink of sin and corruption and evil here so strongly that it would sicken the Evil One himself. You see, as a minister of the Lord, I must always choose to roost where my unique gifts are most sorely needed.'

He made a sudden gesture that had some of the closer drinkers backing up nervously.

'Let the godly rejoice and the purveyors of criminality and perversion beware. The Preacher has come to dwell amongst you!'

A hardened drinker and also a sinner of some scope, blanched at this.

'You . . . you're fixin' to stay here . . . permanent, pilgrim?'

'Preacher to you. And you shall address me as such. But in answer to your question . . . yes, I am staying. And well might you look alarmed, you poor misbegotten apology for one of God's lesser creations.'

He swung back to Malleroy.

'And you, sir, and others of your repulsive profession, shall all too soon discover that I make an implacable enemy as a man whose sinews and heart become as of iron in the battle against all those who plunder the Lord's treasury of immortal souls. So, goodnight to you all. I would add "God bless" but that would be blasphemous under this roof!'

As he swung his back, the man with the stovepipe hat, Leander Kelp, rushed to the swinging doors and held them. Doone went striding out, leaving confusion and curiosity in his dust.

They were accustomed to the new and unusual in Wagontown, but this one had to be some kind of original.

Malleroy was still standing by the doors and scratching his head a short time later when Carmody sought him out.

'Come on, Rand, I'll buy you a shot. You look like you could stand a stiff one.'

The saloonkeeper accepted with alacrity, for he was indeed in need of something strong. Then the stampede to the bar began as everybody realized they needed a drink.

CHAPTER 5

SAINTS AND SINNERS

The arrival of the Preacher hit Wagontown like a Midwest twister.

Within the space of just a few days he had already hit the headlines for various activities ranging from demonstrating his individual style of sinbusting to the rallying of the forces of the God-fearing, or the 'True Believers', as he called them.

As had happened in a score of similar places across a dozen states and territories over the past year and more, this town was at first shocked and stunned by the man's omnipresence and his energy. Yet while some began to mellow and appeared to fall under the spell of his mesmerizing public addresses, many others met together to hatch up plans for ridding the town of his unsettling presence. These plots never materialized, or at least not during that first turbulent week.

'I am the life, the good news, the bringer of the

Word!' he would proclaim, and in no time at all he boasted his own congregation of admirers, even if these largely comprised the Crackers.

The town had given them that name when they'd arrived in late summer from Georgia. Somber and gaunt hill-folk whose drab brown-and-gray garb contrasted sharply with the gaudier hues and glitter of main street Wagontown, the Crackers had gravitated to the poor end of town where they were free to brew up their moonshine and pursue some kind of fundamentalist religion which, as was discovered, seemed essentially very similar to the preacher's own.

'Thet man is a livin' saint,' a brown-skinned mother of three assured Ruth Carmody when the women met by chance on the streets one day. 'He sees the light and he loves us, which is more than can be said for all you high and mighty uppity town folks. The preacher is a-gonna bust all the temples of Sodom and Gomorrah in this here town, woman, so best you warn that man of yours to start in keepin' that newspaper of his'n clean and decent otherwise he'll feel the wrath, sure as death.'

Ruth Carmody was a strong woman. She was not fearful for herself and at first considered not recounting the incident to her husband. But her conscience troubled her. What if she failed to warn Ash, and some evil befell him?

So she told him. His response was typical.

He laughed.

'Ash, this is serious!'

'Of course it is,' he replied, sobering. 'Or could be

if we let it be.' He took her by the shoulders. 'Don't you see, honey? This kind of caper is as old as the printing-press itself. A good newspaper tries always to print the truth, and there are people who hate the truth and will do just about anything to try and suppress it.'

'But surely the preacher is different from others . . . For one, he's a man of the cloth, and he also—'

'He's a charlatan, Ruth.'

'What?'

'Look, I know he's impressive and certainly has zeal. I also know that a lot of respectable women in town have started attending his services, and bringing him food and donations. He's kind to kids and some of the poor folks he's laid hands on have seemed to pick up. But despite all that the man is still no good, and perhaps even dangerous. That will come out one day. In the meantime we've got to put up with him, but not let him weaken us. We're right and he's wrong, simple as that.'

'If you say so . . .'

'Still not convinced, eh?'

'Darling . . . ?'

'Huh?'

'What do you think Doone really wants here in Wagontown?'

'Why . . . success, adulation, money, power. How would I know what motivates these cranks? Why do you ask, Ruth?'

'There's something about him that scares me.

Once or twice I've seen him standing on a corner or in a doorway where he thinks nobody is around, and I have caught him staring at every man who passes by with this terrible sort of suspicion and hatred in his eyes. I . . . I just don't believe it's just the saving of souls, as he claims, or the opportunity to rob and deceive them, as you and others say, that brought him here. There's something more to him than that, I'm sure of it. Something sinister.'

'Know what I'm sure of?'

'What?'

'That you need a day away from responsibilities and Wagontown. Come on, I'll leave my man in charge and we're driving out to Morgan's River for a picnic.'

'But—'

'No buts. Who's the head of this household, Mrs Carmody?'

She laughed. 'Why, me, of course.'

'Of course,' he yelled, lifting her and swinging her in a circle. 'But I'll keep this up until you say you'll go pack the basket.'

Leander Kelp closed his spyglass with a snap. Dust from the river trail floated slowly down out of the sky as the sulky receded over a grassy rise.

Handsome men and pretty women were the bane of his life. He could never be the former, could never attract the latter.

But he doubted he'd even bother reporting to his master that he'd just seen the newspaperman and his wife wheeling out to the river. The preacher demanded he watch every remotely possible potential suspect male in town in the hope of picking up something, anything that might link someone here to a fatal knife-fight in Cairo a year and a half earlier.

He had other more promising suspects to concentrate on today, as he told himself as he made his way back to his horse hidden in the brush.

For instance, high-rolling Honest John Marchant struck him as a man who'd shiv his own mother for a dime. Of course, he appeared somewhat older and heavier than the description of the killers the preacher had been given by that hag back in Cairo.

But what about Otis the night-carter?

Again he shook his head as he rode back towards the town. He had better stop guessing and come up with something the preacher might be able to use, even if it did seem to him like searching for a needle in a haystack.

The donations were beginning to roll in yet the preacher's overheads were high. He was renting a hall for his nightly meetings and attendances were increasing. But hotel rates were steep, so he went looking for something else in the way of lodgings and found it unexpectedly at the white-painted Glory House on tree-shaded Creek Street about half a mile from the town center.

Attracted by the name initially, he investigated to discover that the converted hay barn was a low-rent roomer operated by the Crackers, that strange bunch of Georgians currently taking a beating in the pages of the *Western Globe* over their extremist views on practically everything.

It proved to be a gloomy place with strict rules of conduct and sparse patronage, for thirsty cowboys in from the spreads and visiting firemen preferred brighter and racier places to lay their heads. But it was ideal for this man of the cloth, a refuge where he could rest, reflect, pray – and possibly avoid the enemies he inevitably made no matter where he traveled.

His all-out attacks on the temples of vice and corruption weren't confined to the Two Bits saloon or the Lucky Dice. He spread his net wider every day, his purpose twofold. One, his passion to spread the Word was genuine even if his sermons were heavily overladen with fire and brimstone and eternal torment in the charnel houses of Satan's hell.

But a second and equally strong motivation was the need to raise the dust, to unsettle people and institutions, to disturb the normal and the everyday in this big town in the hope that sooner or later somebody might be rattled into making some error that might lead him to the people he hunted.

But he knew he was no closer to the Cairo killers tonight than on the day he rode in. He was suspicious of everybody but nobody in particular. He couldn't yet begin to calculate just how many Westbounders had ended up in this wide-open outpost on the plains. For the average Wagontowner seemed to view that episode as ancient history, and besides, who cared who came how or when? This was the real West, and everyone was too busy concentrating on the present and the future to be even vaguely interested in the past.

That afternoon he took himself off to the Lucky Dice, not to berate the sinners or harass Honest John but rather to avail himself of the lush desserts available in the supper room that led off the main barroom.

He settled down into a well-upholstered chair at a table for one where his order was taken by a buxom young woman who wasn't wearing one inch more clothing than was required by law.

The preacher sniffed but refused to say anything. He felt a little leg-weary but strong, as was always the case. And seated there, sipping sarsaparilla, he had no sixth sense of danger as he idly watched a fat man in a yellow shirt set up a fresh barrel of whiskey behind the bar. The barman winked at him. He'd been warned not to antagonize the town's flamboyant newcomer until Marchant had made a decision on what was to be done about him. The owner of the Lucky Dice never tolerated either troublemakers or critics for too long.

Turning away, the barman saw the stranger who'd come to lean against the corner of the bar in the half-shadows.

Not one of Honest John's regulars, was the man's first thought. The second was that he thought he looked dangerous somehow.

He sighed. Was he just getting older or were the

72

men coming through the batwings really getting worse?

He concentrated on his work, business began building up and in time he forgot about both the preacher on one side of the long bar and the stranger on the other.

Doone finished his excellent meal in peace, paid his bill, then saw that the saucy girl had gone round the bar and now stood talking to the mean-looking fellow in the corner, one hand on her hip, smiling all over her face and leaning forwards to give him a good look.

Times like this the preacher couldn't help himself.

If he stayed here long enough, people would get to realize that he simply could not keep away from bars, brothels, beer joints or gambling-houses.

The reason for this obsession with such places was simple. They represented the total opposite of everything he believed in and, indeed, had devoted his life to – until something happened in that life to give him a different, darker motivation.

He stared across at Leander Kelp, seated at a bar table with a glass of sarsaparilla before him, waiting for him to finish. He sighted the big flashy figure of Marchant over by the poker layout, but that didn't deter him either.

He didn't raise his voice; didn't really wish to make a scene and maybe spoil his digestion. He simply crossed to the corner and gave the percenter a short lecture on how she should dress, behave and live, barely aware of the man in the half-shadows.

The man was aware of him now.

He was tall and lean, a stranger in town. He'd had three drinks alone at his quiet end of the bar, greasy hat tipped forward over his eyes; buckskinned, iron-toting, unshaven and flinty-looking.

He stared unblinkingly at the towering figure of the preacher and listened to his denunciation of loose living, working in saloons and trying to pick up men in bars.

His eyes turned cold.

His name was Coley Dukes and he'd once been married to a woman who had caught religion the way others might catch cold. She'd made his life into his own private hell until she drove him too far and he drew his gun and shot her dead before hitting the drifter's trail.

Sermonizing preachers had been high on his hate list ever since. This one seemed worse than most.

He leaned forward into the light and threw the contents of his whiskey glass full into Doone's face.

The bar went still. Leander Kelp turned ashen beneath his ridiculous high hat. The barman in the yellow shirt debated whether to involve himself or duck from sight. The preacher quit talking while the girl snatched up her skirts and bolted for the kitchen. Calmly taking a handkerchief from his coat pocket, he sopped up the liquor on his face, his eyes not leaving Dukes's bitter face once.

'Why did you do that, stranger?'

'I don't need any freakin' reason.'

'You really should have one, you know?'

74

'OK. I just can't stomach psalm-singin', gospel-spruikin' sons of bitches like you, is why.'

The preacher replaced the kerchief neatly in his breast pocket.

'You'd like me to leave, I take it?'

'That's goddamn right. If there's one place left on earth where a man should be free of you mewlin' holy-rollers, it's in a bar.' He paused, frowned. 'So, why are you still here, God-botherer?'

Doone stood very straight as he said distinctly:

'I fear you'll have to put me out if that's what you want.'

Now the bartender did disappear. The words halted Dukes for a moment, but not longer. He dropped a hand to the handle of the Remington he wore thonged down on his right hip.

'You're bettin' on a busted flush, big man. I'd as soon shoot one of you soul-savers as not.'

Doone's black coat was buttoned. Deliberately he undid it and hooked the right hand panel behind the Colt resting snug in its polished black holster. For the first time, Coley Dukes's face betrayed a glimmer of uncertainty.

His right arm now crooked out a little from his side, Doone said in the same level voice:

'A man's life is given him by the Almighty. He has a right to protect it. Even a minister of the Lord has that right. So go ahead, you whiskey-drinking scum, make your play if you will.'

Indecision grabbed Coley Dukes so fiercely it made him gasp. Nothing added up here. Here was a

man with a cross at his throat who spruiked like a sin-
buster – and then showed you he's packing iron!
He'd never expected either the aggression or the
Colt. But then, his hand was still wrapped around his
gun handle while the preacher's was clear. Nobody
could hand him that kind of an advantage. Nobody.

Someone loomed up in the corner of the hardcase's vision. It was the law. Shelby had sized the situation up from across the room, and immediately
stepped forward to place himself between the
bristling pair.

'Take your hand off that piece, mister,' he warned
Dukes.

Secretly relieved, Dukes did exactly as ordered.

'Only too happy, Sheriff.'

'All right,' Shelby said, glancing from one to the
other. 'What happened here?'

They told him. Shelby deliberated a moment,
stroking his chin.

'We haven't met,' he said to Doone, 'but I've
heard about you already, reverend. . . .'

'That's Preacher.'

'Whatever. I heard you were heading here, and
after what took place last night, I didn't hesitate to
horn in now, just in case you were readying for more
mischief.'

'There was no real need,' Doone said loftily. 'This
situation would have resolved itself.'

'With guns? Is that how preachers solve their
differences these days?'

'I, Sheriff, am no cringing, white-fingered theology student who faints at the sound of a rude word. This is a violent country and I am committed to bring the Word to it. The Lord himself did not spare the money-lenders; nor shall I flinch from confrontation with whiskey-bemused scum like this.'

Coley Dukes growled like a dog, but Shelby silenced him.

'Quit that kind of talk, Preacher,' he warned. 'This ruckus is over.'

'On the contrary, sir. This cretin did violence to my person. Abuse me and you abuse the Lord. I demand an apology.'

'Better give the man what he wants, Dukes.'

'He had it comin'. No apology.'

'In that case, you can haul your freight and ride out, hardcase.'

Dukes was aggrieved. 'You're runnin' me out of town?'

'You started the trouble, you pay the toll.'

Dukes held his ground for a long moment before dashing his glass to the floor and heading for the exit. Shelby trailed him as far as the batwings and watched until he'd mounted up and headed off along the street. Only then did he return to the glowering Doone.

'First time I ever had to bust up a ruckus between anybody and a man of the cloth,' he remarked drily.

'You may find that as time goes by there may well be many things you will be doing for the first time now I am part of your community, Sheriff. I never allow things to remain as they are. I shall bring change to Wagontown.'

'Well, all settled here?' Marchant said, joining the group. 'It had goddamn better be.' The saloon-keeper put a hard eye on the preacher, who gave him look for look.

'There'll be no more trouble, John,' Shelby said pointedly, eyeing the tall man. 'That's right, isn't it, Preacher Doone?'

The glitter in the preacher's eye was beginning to fade. But his wrath had been genuine. Although here primarily to track down a killer – or killers – his role as a driven spiritual leader was constant and at least equally important to him.

'I decide what is right or wrong,' came the arrogant response.

With that, Doone made to stride off, accidentally bumping Shelby, who reached up quickly and grabbed his bad arm with a grimace of pain.

'Forgive me, citizen,' Doone said. Then he paused with a frown. 'You carry an injury of some kind?'

'It's an old one. I'll be fine.'

Beckoning Kelp, Doone continued for the exit, where he halted before a nervous doorman.

'What's wrong with the sheriff's arm, fellow?'

The man shrugged. 'Dunno. He's had it ever since I been here. Why?'

Without reply, Doone shouldered through the swinging doors with Kelp trailing like the little lapdog he was. On the porch, the big man paused to glance back.

'What is it, Preacher?' Kelp's voice shook. He

loved the *donner und blitzen* of violence, but only from a distance. He'd anticipated gunplay minutes ago.

'Injured arm . . .' Doone murmured as though thinking aloud. 'A man could easily injure a limb in a knife fight, I believe.' He snapped his fingers. 'Come. I believe it's suppertime at the Glory House.'

Ash Carmody splashed cold water over his face at the washstand in the annexe off the printing-room. He allowed the water to drip off as he stood studying his image in the glass. He looked as if he was sweating heavily, realized he had been so back at the saloon.

How could a pleasant afternoon and evening change so quickly from peace to pending violence?

He grabbed up a towel and patted himself dry as he wandered thoughtfully out into the printery, where his man was hard at work, as usual.

Although not always a highly moral man, he seemed to have acquired a certain strong social conscience since taking over the *Globe*. He supposed it went with the territory. Any newspaperman worth his salt set out to improve the society he moved in – encouraging the weak and the poor and at least showing himself ready to hammer the crooked and the criminal.

Dropping into a chair by the desk, he lighted a cigarette and leaned back to blow smoke at the ceiling. He analyzed what had taken place at the Lucky Dice. The new preacher had clashed with some hardcase there, and from what he'd heard it had only been Shelby's intervention that had prevented gunplay.

Before, the man who represented himself as a man of God had smashed a man unconscious at the Two Bits; he'd seen it happen and had felt the danger coming off Deacon Ethan Doone like heat from a skillet.

Some even claimed Honest John Marchant was actually scared of Doone and was considering selling out because of this.

What breed of man of the cloth went about beating up on folks and looking ready to shoot it out with somebody over next to nothing at all! Surely that was exactly the very kind of peculiarly Western insanity a man in his position of influence should respond to and try to change.

He swivelled his chair to face the desk and drew a pen from the holder. It was editorial time again.

CHAPTER 6

THE PAST REMEMBERED

The big man of Wagontown was angry.

'What the hell do you mean by this, Carmody, you back-stabbing, lying son of a whore?'

Ash Carmody leaned back in his chair and linked his fingers across his waistcoat, calmly meeting Marchant's glare.

In back of the bulky figure, Carmody glimpsed four of the Lucky Dice's dealers and doormen along with a personal bodyguard, a lean-flanked punk with a bad reputation.

He was outnumbered. All he had to support him was Dobie Hanrohan who, he noticed only now, seemed to have disappeared at the first whiff of trouble.

'You're referring to the latest edition, I take it, Marchant?' he said easily. The man didn't scare him.

81

It was his belief that no committed Western newsman could afford to let himself be scared.

'I've warned you, mister. What does it take to get through to you that I won't sit back and let you take pot-shots at me that can damage my reputation and maybe even jeopardize several large business projects I have in the planning stages.'

'You mean, like more crooked places like the Dice? And money-lending operations where you screw the poor? Then there's the rumor that you've been juggling the council books in order to evade your land taxes and—'

'You gonna just stand there and take this from this pen-pusher, boss?'

It was the gun punk, backing his challenge with a sneer.

'Ahh, Mr Kipp,' Ash said, getting up. 'Would you be the same Billy Kipp I checked out with Head Office in Wichita, and found out you've got a record in Arkansas for gunplay, standover work and the possible involvement in a murder down there?'

Billy Kipp paled, as did his employer. As part of his climb to power, Honest John Marchant had discovered early that he required personnel of a certain type with quiet consciences and ready fists or guns. Thorough and careful in his recruiting as he was in other aspects of his assorted professions, he'd mostly imported personnel from outside Kansas to minimize the risk of unsavory records coming to the surface.

'Just what are you, Carmody?' he said defensively,

losing his bluster. 'A greenhorn newsman or some kind of bush detective?'

'Meaning I'm right about Billy boy, then, Mr Marchant?'

Marchant had turned a bad color. His pudgy fists clenched and unclenched at his sides. He'd been offended and he had brought along more than enough muscle to handle just one tall newspaper-man. But the truth of the situation was that several bad-smelling, adverse word-of-mouth criticisms and gossip combined with a situation where he was fight-ing to interest some sensitive out-of-town finance in a major development here warned him that if he couldn't bluff Carmody, right now he simply could not afford maybe to put him in the hospital.

'You stinking, one-eyed word-counting—'

'Take it easy,' Carmody said with a smile, realizing he'd called the gambler's bluff, and won. He spread his hands. 'You take things too personal. Sure, I crit-icized you in the latest edition. But you weren't the *Globe*'s only target. I made a strong point that the sheriff should clamp down on main-street hooligan-ism Saturday nights, and my page one editorial was not aimed at yourself but rather our new preacher.'

Marchant began to swear again before curiosity held him. He frowned suspiciously.

'Yeah, what *is* the story on that holy freak anyway? Did you know he's taken to stopping by at the Dice to tell the girls to dress proper and my croupiers to deal straight cards and stop using loaded dice. And, you know something else? I swear that when I tell my boys to kick his holy ass out the door, the psalm-singer acts like he's ready to take them on.'

'I know,' Ash said thoughtfully. 'I've seen him in action. I guess that's why I took a swipe at him. He doesn't ring true, and that's always a concern with anyone who comes to a town. With you, I guess I know what I'm up against, but—'

'Meaning?' Marchant was prickly again.

Carmody shot the man a look of rueful amusement.

'Meaning you're a crook, Mr Mayor. I'm sorry, but I have to call a spade a spade.'

Before Marchant could respond, his man guarding the door spoke sharply.

'And where the hell do you think you're going, feller?'

'Step aside!'

The deep voice outside sounded familiar somehow. Next instant the Marchant man was seized by his shoulders and heaved to one side to make way for Preacher Doone to come striding into the room.

'Out!' he shouted, jerking a thumb over his shoulder. His black-eyed glare focused on a startled Marchant first, but quickly transferred to the boy gunpacker, who was backing away with his right hand hovering over gun handle.

'Go ahead!' Doone's voice was suddenly totally calm. He unbuttoned his black coat, then allowed both hands to drop at his sides. 'Do not start a thing then go to water in the same breath, you mewling, puking mother's boy. You're carrying guns, use them if you—'

'Enough, goddamnit, enough!' Carmody said loudly, stepping between them. 'What sort of craziness is this?'

'You're right . . . you're absolutely right, Carmody,' said a pale-faced Marchant, obviously off-balanced by the sudden rush of unexpected events. He glared at his gunman. 'Kipp! Get the hell outside, and the rest of you with him.'

He waited until his order was obeyed before swinging back to the preacher. Doone had folded his arms and seemed to be calmly half-smiling.

'As for you, you crazy, quack turn-collar—'

'I reckon that might do it, Mr Marchant,' cut in a relieved Ash Carmody. He gestured at the doorway. 'Look, you've made your objection and I'll take note of it. Don't let me hold you up.'

Obviously as eager to be gone as Carmody was to see him go, Marchant settled for a parting glare of warning at the preacher and strode out with some dignity.

The sound of slow clapping filled the printing-office.

'Well done, newsman.' Doone's tone was mocking. 'You do really play the role of the fearless frontier newsman carrying the banner of truth aloft very well. I am impressed.'

'I'm not.'

The clapping ceased.

'Not impressed, sir. With what?'

Ash didn't answer immediately. Instead he went to his desk and took out a box of short sixes. He lit one and flicked out the match. His hands were steady, despite the fact that, yet again in this man's company, he'd just witnessed another incident where gunplay could well have been the outcome.

This disturbed him, angered him. He didn't see himself as any kind of crusader of the press, as his visitor had implied. Yet he was aware that he'd changed since taking over the newspaper and committing himself to both its success and its integrity. Wagontown was a good town, by Western standards, and he wanted to see it advance and progress as such. He genuinely believed Marchant and his pursuits were inimical to this standard, but was beginning also to have serious doubts about Preacher Ethan Doone in this regard.

He sat down, blew a smoke ring and motioned the man to be seated. He remained standing. Carmody shrugged.

'I gather you came to protest against my article. This seems the day for it, so why don't you go ahead?'

'You're a cool one, newsman.'

Ash shrugged, made no reply.

'You're also tall and limber, so I notice.'

He looked up sharply. 'What?'

'Oh, forgive me. I'm quite a student of physical types, you know. Just as I'm fascinated by other aspects of the West, such as, well ... immigration patterns and the reasons and ambitions that drive them, for instance.'

Carmody frowned.

'I thought you wanted to discuss the article.'

'I certainly did . . . originally.' The man grabbed a chair, turned it about then sat with long arms leaning on the backrest. He made a sweeping gesture. 'This scene that just took place here showed me anew just how unique and exciting is this era we happen to be living in. This vast surge of men and women packing their hopes and dreams in boxes and casting off all their ties to board wagon trains and commit themselves to the great adventure . . . I understand you're only recently come to Wagontown yourself, Mr Carmody?'

Ash wasn't sure where this conversation was heading now. Yet he was wary. Indeed he'd been that way ever since a murderous experience on the banks of the Mississippi River had changed his life. It was an attitude he shared with two friends. He'd never forgotten that murdered man and knew he never would.

He had never expected any repercussions from that evil night to catch up with him. But it remained something none of them ever discussed other than occasionally amongst themselves. It made him vaguely uneasy that this strange and curiously dangerous-seeming man should have brought up the matter of the train, no matter how casually.

'Yes,' he said shortly, rising. 'Now if there's nothing else, Preacher, I have business to attend to.'

Doone remained seated, eyebrows hooked up as he watched him move about the cluttered office.

'I would take it as a personal favor if you would help swell my knowledge of the great migration by humoring me and telling me a little more about—'

'Are you a gunfighter, Preacher?'

The question startled the man. He jumped to his feet, features darkening.

'I beg your pardon, sir? Damn your impudence! How dare you ask such a thing of a man of the faith?'

'You dare ask me personal questions. Tell you what, you tell me all about your history and the circumstances that shaped you into a man of God, who looks and acts like some kind of a menace, and then perhaps I'll answer your personal questions. Perhaps.'

For a short space it was still, Carmody watching warring emotions chase one another across that powerful face. But once again Preacher Doone proved capable of self-control. The man forced a grin and brushed long fingers through his graying mane.

'I'm truly sorry to have offended you, newsman. I was not aware that the subject of your western journey might prove so unusually sensitive.'

'It isn't. Now, if there's nothing more . . . ?'

The preacherman left without another word, tall in the doorway as he disappeared. Carmody didn't move for a long minute. He felt he'd handled the matter effectively enough, yet could not be certain that he hadn't overreacted just a little. That in itself should not be any cause for concern, if the man's question had really been as innocent as he'd insisted. But how might his response be interpreted if there had been something more behind Doone's curiosity than the man had admitted?

Footsteps outside. It was Dobie returning from wherever he'd ducked off to when things had begun getting tense. When the man came in he found his boss puffing on a short six and feeding type into the Weisburger. They didn't discuss the sequence of visitors but that didn't prevent Ash Carmody thinking about them long and hard.

CHAPTER 7

THE LIST

There it was again – that strange slapping sound coming through the closed door of the Glory House's most recently rented room, namely Number 7, their best, which the mistress had insisted on giving to the preacher.

The Georgian woman whose job it was to keep the rental wing in immaculate order paused at the door and listened intently, pail in hand, cleaning-cloth slung over her shoulder.

She heard it again and thought she could identify it this time. It was like the slapping sound was followed by a sharp metallic click, then a pause before it was repeated.

Suddenly all sounds ceased. Starting guiltily, the drab woman turned to move off. She knew she'd be in trouble with the mistress were she caught eavesdropping. As well, the guest in Room No 7, Preacher Doone, intimidated her even though he was a man of the cloth and quite the most remarkable speaker she'd ever encountered.

She hadn't taken two steps before the door opened with a rush of air and there he was, bobbing his head to avoid cracking it on the lintel, black eyes drilling at her firstly with suspicion, which instantly changed to a twinkle.

'Dear lady. Slaving in the hour set aside for prayer and feasting?' So saying he grabbed her pail, set it against the wall, removed her cleaning-cloth then took her gallantly by the elbow. 'Come, join me at the table. Today I speak of Sodom and Gomorrah, or to be more precise, this sin-ridden city of Wagontown.'

'Whatever you say, Reverend.'

'Preacher, dear lady, Preacher. I am the Preacher, yet I confess by all the unimaginable glories of Heaven above, that today I come to table with an appetite that would be deemed sinful were my hunger not acquired in the services of my Divine Master.'

The woman blushed. She was a semi-illiterate from the backblocks of Georgia. Yet she was devout and felt a shy pride to be sharing the honor of this man's company as he steered her along the passageway for the dining room.

They entered the long rectangular room which normally seated only some six or seven most days. Today most of the twenty chairs were filled. The cleaning woman was taken aback by the numbers, but the man steering her to her seat alongside his at the head of the table acted as though this jump in attendance was nothing more than he expected.

This happened to be the case. For this was familiar stuff to Preacher Doone. He could land in some backwater town mired in sex, sin and outlawry, where religion was anathema and travelling preachers unheard of, yet within just a few days they would be flocking to hear him speak, even if his theme might be the complete denunciation of his audience and its way of life.

Word of his eloquence and those hard-to-believe rumors of his visits to several of the big saloons had already swept the town. The rejects and the have-nots of Wagontown were not slow to realize that in the space of a couple of weeks they had acquired a voice and a focal point for their resentments against the world in the man of the cloth.

Doone saw at a glance that, although regular town-ers made up about one third of the crowd, the major-ity belonged to the Georgia Cracker society.

He nodded in approval as he set about his steak and vegetables like a starving man.

Wherever he traveled – both prior to his quest and subsequently – he attracted devotees. He always encouraged them, the more fanatical the better. It was his belief that there was no such thing as too much enthusiasm when it came to the accomplish-ment of the Lord's work.

On a more practical level, he was aware that by his very nature he was prone to whip up trouble and controversy. A man in his position couldn't have too many supporters in case some fool should jump up onto a packing crate and begin whipping up support to 'get rid of the holy-roller,' as mostly happened, sooner or later wherever he set up shop.

The meal was solid, sensible food prepared and served by the dour Georgian women and eaten mostly in silence.

The moment his repast was finished the preacher banged a fist down on the table and jumped erect, clasped his big brown hands before him and stared at the ceiling.

'Be upstanding and give thanks for what we have received – now!'

They rose, as if lifted by invisible hooks. Doone promptly launched into an immensely long and convoluted grace of thanks.

When that was through he bade them be seated. After demonizing Wagontown as a 'hell-hole of vice, corruption and atheism' in a few well chosen sentences which found great favor with his listeners – who found the town unfriendly, élitist and snobbish – he paused to take a drink and it was time for Kelp to rise from his chair, on cue.

'Pardon me, Preacher Doone, but could you tell us what future you see for this city iffen we don't embrace the Word?' he asked.

'Death, destruction, the murder of the innocents and no sanctuary but the grave!' Doone responded, tossing his mane and whapping a palm with his fist. 'Unless, of course, we unite to change the course this ship of sin has taken and ensure that, by our faith, our efforts and our implacable hatred for Satan and his minions we change it from a hell-hole of sin and selfishness into a heavenly haven where the lion may lie down with the lamb and the worst of the wicked be named, shamed and dealt with in the Saviour's mighty name!'

They shivered with fervour. This was the sort of fundamental Christianity they craved. This was plainly very much for the poor and against the rich, and seemed to evoke the possibility of their ability to force future change.

This virulent attack on their hosts – the men and women of Wagontown – labeled now as 'the worst of the wicked' was a theme Doone would come back to again and again in the days ahead. For he needed his followers to be angry and committed should he need their support in what lay ahead. He played heavily on their sentiments and sympathy when he related the heartbreaking story of an unnamed 'loved one' of his who had perished at the hands of evil men, all of whom would eventually be fittingly punished when exposed.

He dare not say more on that topic at this time for fear of tipping his hand to the guilty whom he sought, should any by chance be harbored here. He restricted himself to urging that all of them – in the Lord's name – keep eyes and ears sharp for anyone, be it the mayor or the town drunk who might unwittingly, boastingly or even drunkenly, so much as hint at the crime and sin of murder in his or her past.

He would include them in his prayers for evermore if they did so.

He was soon referring to everybody present as brother or sister, and by the time the meeting broke up two hours later they were addressing one another in the same way. Already they were looking at their pastor as though he was some kind of Messiah.

Following the meeting Doone took a nap, then late in the afternoon he went searching for a church to accommodate the crowds he now knew he would attract in the wake of his daring attack on their host town.

He had the nerve to begin with the local pastor, which proved a mistake. He was subsequently rejected by others but as Wagontown would soon learn, Preacher Doone never surrendered easily.

A single candle rammed into the neck of a bottle illuminated the squalid room that had once been the front office of the Wagontown slaughterhouse.

From beyond the room where a towering figure sat brooding over a scrap of writing paper with a stub of pencil in his hand, came the sounds of activity as some twenty men, women and children wielded brooms, buckets and mops to clean floors and walls before transforming the whole grubby building with fresh pipeclay.

The slaughterhouse was the preacher's new church.

He sucked a gashed finger-knuckle absently as he tapped his paper with the pencil. He hadn't intended giving the Reverend Middleton a backhander when he'd gone to visit the local minister with a proposal to rent his poorly attended church on Prairie Street to house his rapidly swelling anticipated congregations.

Unfortunately the parson had proved to be a feisty little man who'd denounced him as a 'charlatan, an enemy of true Christianity, a hypocritical man of violence and quite probably a minion of Satan.'

Doone had all but forgotten the incident by this. He was totally preoccupied with other matters, none of which had anything to do with churches, slaughterhouses or preachers with busted mouths.

He had seven names listed on his scrap of paper, each one representing a citizen of this town who could possibly fit the profile of the man or men he was seeking from the past.

His classification was a sketchy one. To fall into his category the man he was seeking needed to be both tall and relatively young, to have been traveling with the Murdock wagon train of late '67, probably in the company of two others of similar age and appearance, plus one other, and to have arrived at this place sometime over the past eighteen months.

He sighed.

How many such lists had he drawn up in how many towns in that year and a half?

Once or twice he'd been next door to certain he was on the scent of his brother's killers, only to have the whole thing collapse when circumstances, times, dates and details proved conclusively that his suspect or suspects could not have been possibly involved in the great crime.

His cheek began to twitch. He had to fight against disappointment. He'd sworn a terrible oath in Cairo to seek out, find and punish his brother's killer no matter what it took or how many reversals he might have to suffer. To achieve that he could never give in to impatience, disappointment or despair.

Some nights he dreamed of that fateful future hour when he would finally name and face his killer and blast him headlong into Hell.

So, once again he patiently scanned his laboriously assembled list of 'suspects'. They read; Tancred, Coulter, Malleroy, DeBerenie, Marsh, Carmody and Bradbury – representing two cowboys, the town photographer, a saloonkeeper, newspaperman, commission agent and the town water-carter.

These were seven men who might roughly fit the descriptions and details he'd secured that rainy night on the Mississippi; the 'suspects' he would concentrate upon here in Wagontown, Kansas. While all the time he was fully aware that, at this very moment, the real murderer could be boarding a windjammer bound for Australia, or lying dead in a boot hill in Texas.

He rose sharply and glanced out into the slaughterhouse before jamming his hat on his head and making for Front Street.

He decided to kick off tonight by taking a closer look at commission agent Marsh. The man wasn't very tall nor young, but according to information had been in Wagontown roughly eighteen months. It felt like grabbing at straws, but that was better than nothing.

*

The sheriff swayed and the cowboy's fist barely grazed his chin. Off-balanced by the near miss the red-faced waddy lurched awkwardly but was steadied when Shelby slammed his good shoulder into his face with intentional force. The man cursed, cocked his fist again then went down with a crash as the lawman kicked his feet from under and dropped him with a thud that rattled the store windows.

'OK,' Shelby growled to his deputy as the drunk struggled to rise. 'Book him and lock him up to sleep it off. Drunk and disorderly will do.'

Scenes like this invariably drew a crowd. Heads nodded approvingly as the cowboy was hauled away by the husky young deputy who put a hammerlock on him to ensure he didn't get to throw any more punches. There'd been a time when the Circle Ten riders had caused more trouble around town than the miners and railroaders put together. But those days had been numbered the day the mayor pinned the star on Wes Shelby, the quiet man who carried a big stick.

'Well done, Sheriff!' a voice called. Then another chimed in: 'So, when are you gonna move them Crackers on, Shelby?'

Shelby sought out the man, recognized him as a troublemaker. Every town had at least one.

'When and if they break the law, Quinn,' he said sharply. 'Not before.' He gestured. 'All right, break it up. Nothing to see here any longer.'

They obeyed meekly, even the flat-faced Quinn. The sheriff was about to turn away when he realized one had remained in place, standing in the flung shadow of the peppercorn tree, a tall silhouette.

'That goes for you too!' he called. 'No unlawful assemblies in my t—'

He broke off as the figure stepped forward into the light from the store porch. Shelby's broad-boned face tightened. Preacher Doone remained something of an enigma to him, as he was to most. He'd heard the man speak once or twice on street corners, and there could be little doubt that the newcomer was a gifted orator who appeared genuine about his faith and his mission to redeem souls. But he'd also seen Doone in action at the Lucky Dice, knew for a fact that he carried a Colt and had already built a reputation for speaking his mind and rough-handling people who offended him. Made a man wonder just how evangelical he really was.

'Preacher.' He nodded.

'Impressive,' Doone replied, raising a boot to rest it upon the porchboards. 'I'd venture to say that you possess what is known as natural authority, Sheriff Shelby. I must say I would be hard pressed to show such restraint to any whiskey soak who attempted violence upon my person.'

'How would you have dealt with Quinn, Preacher?' Wes asked curiously.

Doone made a very large fist with his right hand and held it up before him like a club.

'The power of the Lord, Sheriff. I would make him

feel it, respect it and fear it. Don't give them a second chance. At the very first transgression, strike first and strike hard. You'd be amazed how much trouble can be saved with scum like that in the long run.'

'Scum? Quinn's just a sodden drunk, man.'

'Preacher.'

'Pardon?'

'I am addressed as Preacher.'

Shelby's jaws tightened at that.

'So, we're being frank and honest with one another. Is that it?'

'I merely reminded you that—'

'All right, let me remind you of something, mister. I run this town by my standards and I don't take kindly to having my rules bent or broken. There have been several incidents involving you that I've let pass mainly because you're newcome and also a man of the cloth. I can see now that lenience may have been a mistake, so I'll make something very clear. From this moment you'll be treated exactly the same as any other troublemaker. Step out of line and you'll end up regretting it. Is that clear enough for you – Preacher?'

Doone's eyes glittered under arched black brows but he bit back his retort with obvious effort. He was anything but intimidated, yet had come searching for information, not conflict.

'Forgive my intemperate tongue, Sheriff Shelby. It's something I've been cursed with all my life. Please allow me to make it up to you. Perhaps we could share a sarsaparilla, or—'

'Don't suck up to me, man,' Shelby cut him off, turning to go. He paused. 'I don't like you, Doone. Call me picky, but a reverend who packs iron doesn't sit right with me. Or one who punches parsons or cons poor dumb hill-folk, either. Yeah, Middleton told me about your assault. That's another reason why I smell fraud or funny in you somewhere. So just remember my warning. You mightn't get another.'

The preacher let a long-held breath escape as he watched the sheriff's figure recede in the direction of the law office. He knew he'd handled the situation poorly; his arrogance and volatility continually complicated his murderous obsession. But he didn't believe in regrets. He'd planned to win the lawman's confidence with the hope of uncovering details on his past history, looking for anything that might link the man with Cairo '67, but had thus far failed completely.

As the situation stood, he'd discovered little more than that Wes Shelby probably shaped up as the most formidable man he'd encountered in Wagontown. A man of his caliber would be capable of killing and concealing it, surely?

It wasn't a lot to go on, but it was enough. Taking out paper and pencil he added the name 'Shelby' to his list of suspects.

CHAPTER 8

'TROUBLE TOWN'

The sun was well down the sky as a shadow fell through the office doorway and Ash Carmody looked up to see the familiar lean figure of Rand Malleroy standing there.

He smiled a greeting and kicked out a chair. The saloonkeeper was always a busy man this time of day, a known fact which caused the editor to raise quizzical eyebrows as his visitor rested a ham on the edge of his cluttered desk and removed his hat. Malleroy's black hair gleamed. He was by nature neat and dapper, rarely worried about anything much, yet it proved to be a troubling concern that had brought him here today.

'That preacher, Ash,' he ventured after pleasantries were exchanged. 'Just what do you make of him, anyhow?'

Carmody didn't have to consider his reply.

'A ticking bomb, Rand.' He grinned. 'How's that

for editorial detachment – I don't think.' He sobered. 'Look, the man's been causing trouble and unrest since day one. I know for a fact he's been feeding his slaughterhouse converts all kinds of rubbish about inequality and fighting for the cause of the Lord and such, and seeding the sort of situation that could easily lead to trouble. But why do you ask?'

'He's been asking questions.'

'What about?'

'About one, two or three relative newcomers who might have come West on a wagon train together eighteen months ago. That's what.'

That brought Carmody up sharp.

'You sure about this, Rand? I know he's nosy and talks too much and acts like everything he does is OK in the eyes of the Lord, but I didn't know . . .' He paused and shook his head as he rose. 'Do you know why he's asking these questions here in Wagontown?'

The other shook his head.

'No notion. But it's put me on edge, Ash, I don't mind telling you. I mean, after all, that was a pretty messy business back in Cairo. Us coming upon that dead man that way then having to hike off to catch the cattle boat before we could find out what it was all about, or help the law or do anything, for that matter. I've got to admit that from time to time I've wondered if there mightn't be repercussions for us from that night some day.'

'It's only sensible you should feel that way, man. But then we knew that all along, didn't we? That's why we've never let on we came west together, or hung around together too much just in case somebody somehow might link us to that business. Tell me, has Wes heard anything along these lines about the preacher?'

'Don't know. I only latched onto it myself today. Thought I'd go check with him after I saw you.' Malleroy half-smiled. 'I figured that you being the newsman with your nose in everybody's business, you might have picked up something on the preacher that might give us a lead on where his curiosity is coming from.'

Carmody stroked his jaw reflectively, then shook his head.

'Sorry, nothing comes readily to mind, Rand. But I can tell you something. From here on in I'll be keeping tabs on our preacherman. We're innocent of any wrongdoing, we've set up good lives for ourselves here and we're not standing by while some holy joe, who acts like a kind of law unto himself half the time, gets to cause us any kind of grief. Just leave it with me. The way I see it, Doone is sailing pretty close to the wind both with the law and the town council as things stand. If I decide he poses some kind of threat to us I won't hesitate to use the power of the press to throw him on the defensive, maybe get rid of him altogether.'

'Good man, Ash.'

They shook hands soberly, two men who shared a secret and a bad memory. Who'd faced peril together before and who would fight to preserve what they'd built in their new home in the West.

*

The only sounds in the room were the rhythmic slap of palm on bone handle, the sibilant hiss of steel as it cleared soft leather, the dry hammer snap on an empty chamber.

The unchanging sequence of sounds had been whispering beneath the closed door into the passageway for a full half-hour. In his austere quarters, with its single bed, bureau, washbasin and chair with a Bible resting upon it, the 'very reverend' Preacher Ethan Doone was practicing his clear and draw.

He stood in the center of the room, coat and vest removed, facing the door. He dropped the gun into the holster, shifted his hand away, then sent it slashing down.

Hand and weapon merged as one and the hammer snapped in almost the same instant that palm smacked gun-handle. The preacher's draw was a thing of perfection, an action of flowing speed and machinelike in its very consistency.

Ethan Doone was a rare breed of gunfighter who didn't really need to practice to maintain his lethal edge. He did so religiously, however, because it made him feel good, reassured him of his temporal power as opposed to the spiritual and reinforced his awareness of his ability to deal with any danger he might happen to confront.

He was a man who might uncomplainingly ride all night through freezing rain to help save a man's soul, but would just as readily undertake the same journey to deal brutally with another man who did him wrong.

He was brooding on the greatest wrong done him nineteen months earlier in a riverside slum far from sunny Kansas, when the discreet tap of knuckles sounded on the door.

'Come!'

Leander Kelp entered.

The preacher nodded and put the big gun away on his hip. Kelp lowered himself to a corner of the bed. The rustling sound reminded him of the newspaper he carried in his hip pocket. He drew it forth and looked up.

'Durn nigh forgot this, Preacher. I kept it to show you.'

'Carmody's trash rag. What's in it?'

'He's got half a page about the last big meetin' at the slaughterhouse, he has.'

'Let me see that.'

Doone read fast. Three nights earlier he'd done such a brilliant job of firing up his largely Cracker audience on the always volatile topics of social inequality, prejudice and Wagontown's pervasive venality and its tolerance of gambling houses and bordellos, that directly afterwards some of the younger males had gone up to Front Street in aggressive mood, resulting in a brawl subsequently broken up by the law.

Now the editor was criticizing the Church of God for fanning religious antagonism and creating social unrest.

Jaw muscles working, he turned the pages and skimmed a second article critical of Honest John Marchant backed up by fresh charges of crooked wheels and dice, and the heavy handedness of the Lucky Dice's doormen.

He flung the paper aside and began pacing the room, three long strides one way, three the other.

Kelp followed his every step, sharp-eyed and eager. He knew the preacher better than anyone, understood the patterns he tended to follow, what pleased and satisfied him and what touched off his trigger temper.

The man who knew Doone best had noticed a change in him in recent days, a sharpening of his moods, a dangerous eagerness in the way he'd suddenly stepped up the pace of his manhunt; the questioning, probing, going over old documents and newspaper files, sniffing the air like a bloodhound.

This change had been brought about by a seemingly casual conversation between Doone and a drunken day laborer who'd come staggering along to the Church of God looking for salvation.

It turned out this derelict had been employed for a time as Ash Carmody's handyman at the newspaper office, and under Doone's by now almost automatic probing, had revealed that both Sheriff Shelby and saloonkeeper Rand Malleroy had been occasional visitors to the *Globe* headquarters in that time, always arriving singly, by the rear entrance and at night.

It was sketchy and insubstantial coming from such an unreliable source who just might have concocted the story to ingratiate himself with an ongoing source of charity grub from the church.

But at least it was something.

Up until the present moment Doone had been unable to secure any confirmation of this piece of 'information'. He was, at the same time, closely monitoring some three or four others whom he had under suspicion, who at this stage all looked somewhat more likely suspects than three of Wagontown's more prominent and successful citizens.

Yet just today he'd fallen to brooding about the three in question, wondering if he might not be getting desperate and trying to fit people into his framework of suspicion. Clutching at straws.

Then suddenly this copy of the *Globe* gave him fresh heart. It seemed at least a possibility that Carmody was suddenly going out of his way to attack him and his church, which could be interpreted as proof that the man might be aware of his intentions and so wanted to be rid of him.

He stopped pacing suddenly. He stood by his little window staring out with what his flunky called his 'thinking look' as he watched a scrawny Cracker woman removing washing from a line.

'Obvious,' he said suddenly, snapping his fingers. 'This could mean a lot or nothing, Kelp. But what it tells me is that it's high time I moved our quest into the next phase. Up until now we've been consolidating, have grown strong, worked day and night for leads which we may or may not have secured. Isn't that so?'

'Huh?'

Much of the time Leander Kelp had little understanding of what the preacher was talking about. He didn't much care. What he loved – and what stimulated his miserable little soul – was the situation which invariably evolved sooner or later wherever they travelled. Namely, when Doone's aggression and and arrogance triggered off resentment and eventually violence. This was the fuel that fired Kelp, and he felt he could smell the first whiff of real trouble in the dusty air of Wagontown right now.

'Pay attention, man!'

'Oh yeah . . . the next phase. Sure, I understand, Preacher Doone. We've been kinda layin' the groundwork, so now it's time to . . . er, get serious?'

'Precisely. It's time to start the mills of God to grinding. I've permitted this town to doze in its atheistic, hedonistic complacency far too long. We have built up considerable strength through my congregation and I now have those inbred Georgians eating out of my palm, right?'

'Er . . . sure you have, Preacher.' Kelp sounded proud. 'They'd do about anything for you and—'

'We'll be subtle,' Doone broke in, hammering a fist into his palm with a smack. 'Right now we need to take this town by the scruff and turn it upside down if we wish to shake out any bad apples. But because the sheriff is one of our persons of growing interest, we shan't tempt fate by overreaching and challenging the law office directly. But we can achieve the same ends by swinging public sentiment against Honest John. Right now that fornicator is smarting under the *Globe*'s latest attack. If I whip up our tame sheep – as I know I can – to support the cry against that man, you can be assured he will react, hopefully with violence. You see? This could be our trigger to destabilize the town, weaken the law's position and thereby give us greater freedom to investigate and possibly uncover our suspects.'

Kelp was on his feet. It was all a little ambitious and complicated for him, but he got the general drift. 'But will the flock dare oppose Honest John the Antichrist and flesh-peddler? Most folks believe he is the real power in town, and our Crackers are—'

'Are mewling sheep who eat out of my hand and who will do whatever I ask of them.'

Kelp nodded slowly. The one thing he never doubted was the preacher's ability to sway a mob. He'd seen him do it a dozen times. He was stirred as he always was by the prospect of sweet violence, but, as usual at such times, fearful. He would love to see blood running in the gutters of Wagontown, providing it wasn't his.

Yet when he looked at the deacon standing there seemingly so implacable and invincible, his fears began to ebb. The two had seen much trouble together and danger together, virtually all of it incited by Doone. But they'd always emerged relatively unscathed. Doone was too fierce, fast and ruthless for any man, possibly for any town. He saw no reason why he couldn't take Wagontown apart and survive as he'd done before. Sometimes this creepy little boot-licker actually believed that God really was on Preacher Doone's side.

'So, call a meeting for tonight and issue a special invitation for our Georgian brothers and sisters to attend.' Doone's eyes glittered with genuine excitement. 'It's time. This smug, fat community is about to be shaken loose of its moorings when they confront the power of the Word carried to their evil doorsteps by all the true believers!'

He raised his fists and hammered the ceiling, bringing down a fine film of plaster.

'The day of the Lord is at hand and if it is his divine will, chaos shall lead to purification of the sinner and our sacred revenge!'

'Amen, Preacher! Amen and alleluia!'

Flanagan the blacksmith glanced up from his forge as his eye caught movement just beyond the fireglow – a tall, dark-garbed figure striding by at a pace he would have been unable to match even if running.

'Glad to see someone still with fuel in his boiler at the fag-end of a hard day,' he muttered sourly. 'Who was it anyway, boy? Dressed kinda funny, wasn't he?'

'Always is, Mr Flanagan,' replied his grease-grimed striker. 'It were him. You know? The preacher.'

'That one?' the smith's voice was thick with disapproval. He turned his head and spat. 'Wonder what lit a burr under his tail?'

'Strange one that, boss.'

'Strange? Seems I could think of somethin' more descriptive than that if I put my mind to it. C'mon, turn that shoe over. Some of us got honest work to do, just like there's them that don't do a hand's turn but pray and spruik and fill dumb folks heads full of loco notions.'

Further along Main Street other heads turned as a by now familiar figure in black strode on by, long legs eating up distance, burning eyes occasionally flashing from hat-brim shadow as he passed beneath the lights.

The preacher was riding a streak.

Ever since his arrival in Wagontown he'd held himself in check, although this certainly wasn't the way the man in the street saw him. He kept reminding himself he was here on a mission, that focus and self-discipline were the qualities he must project in order to build up his reputation and impress the followers whom he might have to call upon before he was through here.

But tonight was different. Things were moving and he was making them move. He seriously doubted that the flimsy suspicion he'd bestowed on three prominent citizens might bear fruit. But it was something after weeks of nothing. In one and a half hours he was due to mount the impromptu stage in the old slaughterhouse and whip up the drones against the town's most powerful citizen. Sparks should fly as a result and he would be there to fan the flame.

He paused at a fence where a crude hand-painted sign advertising tonight's 'prayer crusade – special topic, Dens of the Devil.'

If Mr Big didn't realize that meant him, he was not as smart as he thought he was. And in his heightened frame of mind, the preacher knew he couldn't resist seeing just how Honest John might be taking it.

He entered the Lucky Dice from the horse yard and took a rear corridor through to the cheap bar where the day laborers and handymen drank beer while the more affluent knocked back the rum, rye and brandy in the main bar and gaming room.

Drinkers stared at him suspiciously as he took a chair by an archway offering a view of the larger room. It was crowded and noisy and, with his hat tugged low over his face, Doone soon sighted Marchant's familiar bulky, smooth-faced figure holding court over by the poker layout.

Mr Big looked sore.

Doone smiled wolfishly, then glanced up as something young and nubile emerged from the writhing clouds of cheap tobacco smoke at his side.

'OK, what'll it be, Reverend?'

'You're half-naked,' he replied.

'At least I don't wear a big hat indoors, do I?' the girl replied tartly. 'Do you want a beer or are you just hear to leer at the tits and legs?'

He flushed and bit back a fierce retort. He had to remind himself he was only here to observe and to enjoy the spectacle of tonight's target trying to figure out why he'd suddenly become of interest to the Church of God.

'Begone!' he snapped, his stare so fierce that even the thick-skinned little percenter was finally intimidated, leaving him without one of her trademark put-downs.

He turned to realize that Marchant and his party seemed to have stopped talking and were staring in his general direction, even though he knew they couldn't see him in his shadowy corner.

But he'd been spotted.

He rose immediately. He'd gotten what he'd come for and had no interest in causing a ruckus here where the odds were so high.

He halted abruptly. Two men stood before him. Their shoulders were wide and their eyes blank. Had he come upon them in the middle of Death Valley he would have recognized them instantly as saloon heavies.

'Peace be with you,' he murmured, and made to step around them. The larger of the pair moved to block his path. He had eyes like bullets.

'Let's hear your sermon, God-botherer. You know, the one you got advertised. Dens of the Devil.'

'Let me pass.'

'Not until you give us a prayer,' jeered the second man.

'What prayer?'

'Why, the one you say down on your lousy stinking knees, you psalm-singing, back-stabbing son of a bitch!'

It seemed to the onlookers that the preacher lowered his head as if in humble acknowledgment of the fact that he'd blundered badly in coming here on this particular night.

They could not have been more wrong. Inside, Doone was exulting. He inhaled the excitement and felt his mind slip the leash of sober restraint. He saw this situation and opportunity for release in vivid clarity.

He was the preacher, these were faces of the ungodly, his was the power.

He struck without a hint of warning. His pistoning fist smashed the pale poker-face, breaking bones and snapping off teeth. The head-butt that followed sounded like an axe biting teak, and the man's legs collapsed beneath him, bringing him down.

The second man landed on the preacher's back, an arm like steel whipped about his neck to depress his windpipe.

He dropped his head to below knee-level and bucked his big body. The man was flung clear. He crashed onto a table whose legs gave way beneath the sudden weight. The preacher snatched up a splintered chair-leg and rammed it into the doorman's throat. Hot crimson spurted and a woman screamed and fainted. Leaping across the gagging doorman, Doone went through a bunch of stunned drinkers like a snow plough to reach the exit. He whirled to face Marchant and his party as they came rushing in.

They slowed. They thought the towering figure clutching the bloodied piece of wood looked crazy. And maybe he was. Crazed and very dangerous as he opened his dark coat left-handed and dim light winked on metal and leather at his waist.

His voice filled the room:

'As the whirlwind passeth, so is the wicked no more; but the righteous is an everlasting foundation!'

The saloonkeeper, flushed and enraged, choked out:

'Take him!'

Two bruisers started forward, but three held back. But the two propped on a dime when Doone hurled the chair-leg with astonishing force and accuracy to pierce the saloonkeeper's flank and bring him screaming to the floor. He straightened from his crouch and allowed his right hand to drop alongside his gun handle.

In that instant the intruder looked like every saloonman's nightmare – the one you couldn't bluff, who just might be as dangerous as all your muscle put together.

When, after several seconds, the two enforcers turned to look uncertainly at the wounded Marchant, the preacher knew he had triumphed, as almost inevitably he did.

'You fear, and quite rightly so,' he said in his best pulpit voice. 'But think of what you have gained. Had fear not stayed your hand you could all be lying dead in this very moment out of eternity, Marchant. But take my warning and leave this town tonight. For I am the power, the light and lord of life and death. So bow your ugly heads in prayer and vow to mend your ways.' He made the sign of the Cross. 'And God be with you.'

In that moment an eerie sense of unreality seemed to grip the Lucky Dice. This strange man's almost hypnotic personality seemed to hold them in the grip of indecision as they stared from the damage he'd done to his serene, burning-eyed stare that seemed to touch every man and woman individually.

And the bloodless, horrified face of the bleeding saloonkeeper, struggling to rise and slipping in his own blood, told every watcher that Mr Big was all through. Terrified, speechless, he stared at Doone for a long moment in total silence. Suddenly the Preacher turned with a sharp flap of black coat-tails and was gone.

In his private office in back of the cells, Sheriff Shelby changed into a fresh shirt and tied his string tie by the last dregs of daylight. From the mirror the image of his bronzed face looked back at him. He combed his thinning hair, put on his hat and flexed a stiff shoulder before lifting the bottle.

He poured a quarter of an inch of whiskey into a glass, and rinsed it around his mouth before swallowing. He waited for the warmth to hit his belly, and when it did he quit the room and walked through to the front where his deputy sat working on the files.

'Goin' on patrol, Sheriff?'

'Not exactly.' Shelby looked at the patch of street visible through the open door. He frowned. 'I'm going to talk to the preacher, as a matter of fact.'

'Oh. You mean the ruckus . . . ?'

'That I do, Deputy,' he murmured, going out, 'that I do.'

The town seemed quiet in the twilight hour. Peaceful. But the lawman wasn't deceived. The undercurrent was there; you could feel it. It had been noticeable for some time, was sharper tonight than it had been yesterday. Yesterday he'd had two men laid up at Doc Swinton's with injuries sustained in the line of duty. Now Marchant had been hurt, had packed and left town, kicked out by the preacher.

It was three blocks to the former slaughterhouse, now known as the Church of God.

It was his first visit and he was impressed by the changes they'd made. He found a number of Georgian women at work in the meeting hall, preparing for tonight's service. They scowled and offered no greeting. The Crackers had arrived here with chips on their shoulders, poor, downtrodden and largely illiterate. Somehow he was not surprised they had become such ready disciples of the strange preacher from nowhere. He'd heard some of a public sermon Doone had given uptown shortly after his arrival. The man could talk a blue streak. No harm in that. It was some of his other 'talents' that disturbed.

A silent woman vanished inside and mere moments later Doone appeared, hatless, sober and impressive.

'Welcome to my church, Sheriff.'

'You don't appear surprised to see me, Preacher.'

'I was set upon by minions of that flesh-peddler, Marchant, and I did no more or less than defend myself. Now, is there anything else, sir?'

Shelby felt himself flush.

'You put two men in hospital. I could charge you

with malicious assault.'

A cold smile touched Doone's lips. 'What is the real reason you are here, Sheriff? Or might I guess? You'd like to see me gone, wouldn't you? You don't want someone coming along to your town and taking up the cause of the unfortunate and downtrodden. You don't want someone speaking out in public against your icons of greed and debauchery. They'd be putting pressure on you, I know. Bloated money-grubbers and power-seekers. Get rid of the holy-bones. Well, you'll find that not an easy thing to do. But where are my manners? Let me offer you some refreshment. Mrs Jackson, something for my guest, if you please.'

'Forget it.' Shelby was terse. He felt something less than his usual assured self in this man's company, on his turf. 'I'll let you off with a warning this time, Preacher. But I won't tolerate violence in my town. And while I'm here I should tell you that some of your people, mostly the young and unemployed, are behaving rebelliously and offensively up-town. They're trying to shove religion down people's throats and seem to feel they have a right to do it. They don't, and you'd better convince them of that.'

'What happened your shoulder, Sheriff Shelby?'

'What?'

'The damage to your—'

'I heard what you said. What the hell business is my shoulder to you?'

'It seems an innocent enough question to me. Why, is it some great secret?'

'Look, don't worry about my shoulder. Don't worry about anything except the fact that you are treading dangerously close to the borderline in Wagontown, and I will not tolerate any troublemaking in future. Do I make myself clear?'

'Clearer than you might think, Sheriff.'

Shelby left. The preacher stood staring after him. A woman approached with a drink but was waved away. He was still standing there when Kelp appeared and crossed to him. The sheriff's figure was small along the road but still identifiable. The man was surprised to see that Doone was smiling.

'What was that about, Preacher?'

'I'll tell you what it was about. It was about those forces arrayed against our mission rolling out their big guns. They want us gone, Mr Kelp. But why?'

'Guess it had something to do with the trouble at the saloon, Preacher?'

'No, sir, it was everything to do with my success.'

'Preacher?'

By now Doone was almost laughing with pleasure. He gestured.

'Don't you see? I've been probing, pressing, asking questions, searching for clues, leads . . . anything that might connect someone here with my brother's murder. What we just witnessed could well be the proof I've been searching for that there are men here with guilty consciences, something to hide. So, what do these men do? They send the sheriff. But we know for a fact that Sheriff Shelby is a relative newcomer. And if you think on it, he is also tall and still on the right side of thirty.'

'You mean . . . ?'

Doone's smile vanished. 'I mean that what just happened could be the very first indicator I've received in all my time here that our killer or killers might be lurking here, Mr Kelp. I believe that calls for a celebration, don't you?'

Kelp brightened.

'Sure. What kind of celebration, Preacher?'

'Why, a prayer meeting, of course.'

CHAPTER 9

WEAR BLACK FOR
BROTHER IKE

Flanagan the blacksmith punched the Cracker in
the teeth, then grabbed him by the shirt and held
on. Flanagan wasn't hurt, just running short of
breath. His opponent, the man who'd insulted him
outside the saloon by calling him a drunkard, was
lighter, less strong and not half as good a brawler.
But he had youth on his side and Flanagan was
made aware of that when he tore free and head-
butted him.

That did it.

Up until that moment Flanagan had only been
irritated. Now he was mad. Shaking his head clear, he
feinted with his knobby blacksmith's left fist, then
sledged a hard right to the left ear with all his weight
behind it.

The Cracker started walking away on rubbery legs,

out on his feet. But Flanagan was still sore. So he went after his man and brought a rabbit-killer down on the back of his neck. The Georgian hit ground like a sack of dirt.

There'd been nobody else around when the brawl began but suddenly they were coming at him from all angles, yelling and cussing. Flanagan stood his ground and spat in the dust. Of course, they travelled in packs! What else would you expect of a bunch of dogs?

He got the first one with a classic pile-driver right cross straight to the jaw. But as the others came swarming in the blacksmith sensed he might be outnumbered and might come to harm if he didn't swallow his pride and run.

He ducked under a left, dodged a lashing kick, took three long strides towards safety, and crashed headlong into the deputies.

'Mr Flanagan!' the tall one chided while his fellow deputy lined up the Crackers with the aid of his billy-club.

'How can we expect young hot-heads to behave when seniors who should know better—'

'Watch your language, Deputy!' he panted, sleeving sweat off his shining face. 'No seniors here. Just one citizen who'd had about enough of these ... these danged aliens and their bad mouths.'

It didn't take the deputies long to get things settled down. Clashes between towners and Crackers were growing in frequency and they now followed a policy of simply breaking up the fights, issuing warnings and sending the belligerents on their way.

Which suited Flanagan fine.

But, wending his way home, he realized he needed to clean up some before facing Mrs F, so he changed direction and headed for the smithy to clean up and maybe have one last snort from his stash in back of the forge.

He was feeling chipper by the time he approached the shop, which occupied a corner on the opposite side of the street from the *Western Globe* office. Damned Crackers! He didn't have enough religion to fit in a hollow tooth himself, and it rubbed him up the wrong way to have newcomers showing up one week and quoting scripture to a man on the street the next.

The smithy loomed before him, quiet, peaceful and familiar after the turmoil at the saloon. He paused by the side door to squint across Front at the Carmody place, where lights showed brightly, and was about to reach for the latch when he heard it. It wasn't loud or sharp, but he'd definitely heard the sound of someone shifting their weight from one foot to another. And it had come from inside!

He jerked the sheet-iron door open, glimpsed a silhouette, threw up his fists with a curse and next moment was knocked off his feet for the second time in half an hour!

He seized a leg as the dark figure plunged by. He hung on. The man kicked at his head and missed. Flanagan seized the flying leg and sunk his teeth into the ankle.

'Fornicator!' snarled a vaguely familiar voice. A fist whistled by his head but by now the powerful black-smith was hauling himself upright, hanging onto a black coat. An elbow crunched the side of his head. He struck back, and as his fist made contact, saw the face clearly.

He was brawling with Preacher Doone!

He swore in anger and astonishment, the curse cutting off sharply as a fist of iron smacked his teeth and filled his head with shooting stars.

'On your knees!' the voice boomed in his ears and Flanagan went down, not in obedience but because his legs had turned to rubber.

Preacher Doone could hit!

That was his single clear thought for the half minute that followed before he could haul himself erect. He was alone, but not for long. Through blur-ring eyes he could see figures crossing Front Street from the newspaperman's house.

'Well, boys – and you, Mr Flanagan, now that every-thing seems to have settled down, I'll go finish that letter to me mother. Or perhaps you'd like me to get you another poultice for your poor face, Mr Flanagan?'

'Thank you kindly, Ruth.' The blacksmith grinned. 'But your coffee and cake did me more good than any medicine, you'd better believe.'

Ruth kissed the top of Carmody's head where he sat in his leather chair and vanished down the hall-way. For a long moment the four men sat looking at one another, waiting for the sound of the study door closing. Only when they heard the click of the latch did they begin to relax. For Carmody's young wife knew nothing of events of eighteen months ago that had linked three Westbounders and the Wagontown blacksmith in an event that, almost forgotten until some weeks ago, had cast a shadow over all their lives.

Carmody, Shelby and Malleroy rarely got together at one another's homes. Tonight was an exception brought on by the march of recent events, and by sheer coincidence had seen Flanagan, the rough and ready smith they'd palled up with in Cairo, also turn up under very strange circumstances.

Up until that point Flanagan hadn't revealed the identity of the intruder he'd clashed with across at the shop. They'd sensed he knew who it had been; all three were looking at him questioningly now as he sat there looking like he'd been worked over by a couple of fractious horses.

He said in response to the unasked question. 'The goddamn preacher-man.' He fingered the side of his jaw. 'He gave me this lump.'

All three began speaking at once. A sober Carmody called for quiet, then said:

'Doone?'

The blacksmith nodded and Carmody went on:

'He was hiding in your smithy at night-time? What the hell was he doing?'

'I got the hunch he was watching something,' came the reply.

126

'What?' demanded Wes Shelby.

'This house, of course.'

Silent looks passed from one face to another. The blacksmith's words conjured up all sorts of possibilities, none of them encouraging.

For the truth of the matter was that it had been Preacher Doone, the savage brawl at the saloon, and the man's clash with Shelby out at the slaughter-house chapel, that had elevated the spectre of the man in the town to such a degree that the saloon-keeper and the sheriff had gotten together to discuss matters earlier and had decided the situation was serious enough to warrant a discussion with Ash Carmody.

Doone was the reason they'd gotten together. Yet before they'd had the chance to discuss the man, the ruckus had broken out across the street, which viewed in retrospect made it seem very clearly that, while they had gathered to talk about the preacher-man, he'd been there not sixty yards away, spying on them!

But why?

Unless . . .

Looks were exchanged, minds were travelling down similar haunting tracks.

The shadow of Cairo, Kentucky, seemed to envelop the suddenly silent room.

They knew by this that Doone was undoubtedly a clever man, subtle and careful in some respects despite his volatile and even brutal nature in others.

Ever since his arrival in Wagontown the man had been continuously peering, probing, questioning. Not about the town or the spiritual lives of its citizens. He wasn't concerned with politics or women or who turned up at his revivals or who despised him as a charlatan. Subtle as he was with his eternal interrogations, the pattern of them had slowly emerged, and it seemed that the three friends had each begun to recognize it at around the same time.

Questions about new arrivals, wagon-train journeys, settlers' origins, evolving social patterns, close friendships, suspicious behaviour, secrecy, liaisons: such things were plainly the preacher's preoccupations, and in just the last several days or so had begun to loom large in the minds of three comparative newcomers with a shared past.

It was something they had feared in their early days in Wagontown: that due to what had happened, and how, suspicion or blame could possibly be leveled at them. Those fears had faded with time, which made their sudden return all that more traumatic.

What was the preacher's true interest in Cairo? And who was he, really? Might he actually be under cover law of some kind? A manhunter with a brief to track down the killer of a prospector in the river-town's docklands, maybe? Surely it was even possible he was a bounty killer in disguise, looking to bring a suspect in dead or alive for money?

Suddenly all were talking at once. Cigars were lighted, Flanagan helped himself to the whiskey, theories and speculations were aired, rejected, then conjured up again when alternative notions were exposed as faulty.

Then Flanagan, the down-to-earth working man with the no-nonsense attitude, interrupted. He respected men who could produce a newspaper, own and operate a saloon or hold down the risk-laden responsibility of a Western peace officer. None the less, after a while he came to the conclusion that they were really missing the point.

'What you're saying,' he cut in, looking from one to the other, 'is that you're afraid this holy geezer is sniffin' after whoever killed the man we stumbled across in Cairo. And that if he decides it was one or all of us, he'll likely come after us with that six-shooter of his, despite the fact that we're innocent as babies. Is that how it shapes up, or have I got it wrong?'

Three heads nodded. He had it close enough to dead right. By this, Carmody, Shelby and Malleroy regarded Flanagan as a true friend. Eighteen months, and he'd not let out a single whisper here about what had happened one rainy night on the Mississippi. That qualified him as a true friend.

'Then the solution looks simple to me,' the man concluded, finishing off his drink. He set the empty glass back on the small table before him and looked up at them from beneath hooked eyebrows. 'Kill him before he kills you.'

They thought he was joking. He wasn't. The situation was black-and-white to this man.

Wes Shelby was attempting to convince him that what he was proposing was immoral when Ruth reappeared, prettily dressed in a flowing nightgown and holding an envelope.

'I'm off to bed, gentleman,' she said, giving her husband a hug. 'So I'll leave you to whatever important gossiping you've obviously still got to do.' She passed Carmody the letter. 'This came today, honey, I just found it under the door. 'Night all.'

The door closed and Carmody frowned at the envelope. Then he noticed the acronym identifying the sender. N.I.B. News Information Bureau.

'This is what I call timing,' he said, ripping it open. 'A week ago I wrote to contacts I have at the bureau asking what information they might have, if any, on Doone.' He scanned the closely typed page. 'Let's see . . .'

'Well?' Shelby demanded impatiently, after a silence. 'We don't have all night . . .'

'Hell! Talk about pay-dirt,' Carmody said with suppressed excitement. 'Just listen to this . . .'

He got up and began to read:

'Private records show that Ethan Doone, now known as Preacher, was born and reared in North Missouri, son of a sodbuster who was also a lay preacher. Doone first came under the notice of the law when he shot and killed a share-cropper neighbor. Investigation found self-defense. Following that incident, Doone worked as a bounty hunter and built a reputation as a fast gun throughout Montana and Wyoming, and was therefore continually featured in the press—'

'A damned gunslinger . . . !' Flanagan snorted, but Shelby silenced him with a sharp gesture.

'Go on, Ash.' He nodded.

Carmody continued:

'He became lethally skilled with a sidearm but never killed feloniously. He invariably challenged a man, then slew him, fair and square, thus escaping prosecution. Some five years ago his lifelong interest in religion appeared to overtake him. He took up preaching and only occasionally came to notice with his gun. Although still a supposed pastor or evange-list, he is regarded by officialdom with deepest suspi-cion and should be regarded as basically what he has always been, namely a killer!'

He lowered the letter and looked up.

'It's signed by the Bureau Chief, Kansas City. So, where does that leave us now?'

The room was silent for a full half-minute before Wes Shelby cleared his throat.

'Well, we knew the man was trouble from the start, but even I didn't think the trouble was this serious.' He paused to glance around, his expression grave. 'What's to be done? He's committed no punishable crime but it seems certain that that could only be a matter of time. I sure don't fancy the idea of just sitting around until he murders some poor fool. What about the rest of you?'

The discussion that ensued was long and intense. Each man present knew he was settled here for life. Wagontown represented the promised land they'd come seeking; they perceived Ethan Doone as a threat to their new home. Between them, Carmody, Malleroy and Shelby represented significant power in the town, and they debated the wisdom of drawing on that power to force Doone to close up shop and leave. This proposal was debated at length, but ended up with Shelby shaking his head.

'I guess we could make him go, gents, but it wouldn't be strictly legal. I'm afraid we might just have to put up with this man fighting and whipping up the poor folks and running around playing detective about Cairo until he either wearies of it or makes a slip-up he can be nailed on.'

Carmody knew the sheriff's words made sense. But he for one wasn't prepared to leave it at that.

'OK, so we don't want to break the law,' he stated firmly. 'But that doesn't mean we've just got to let Doone run like a wild bronc. We've got legal weapons and we can use them.'

'What sort of weapons are we talking about, man?' Malleroy wanted to know.

'I'm a newspaperman. I'm free to publish my opinions and points of view . . . so every time Doone does or says anything that I object to I've got the weapon to respond. And by God I'll do it!'

'Well said, Ash,' Shelby applauded. 'And the same goes for me. I won't give him any kind of free rein, just because I can't toss him into jail, which I'd like to do. I'll ride herd on him, and that'll give me a lot of pleasure.'

'And I'll be within my rights in throwing the

psalm-singing fraud out of my place any time he looks like making trouble,' Malleroy enthused. 'And he will. He's drawn to saloons because they represent the devil in his eyes. He should talk! There's nothing wrong with our town, no matter what he preaches. Right now, he's the only thing wrong with it. And we have to change that.'

The meeting ended on that positive note. Flanagan applauded the decisions taken, but for some reason didn't sleep well that night. And when he eventually dropped off it was only to have his dreams invaded by a vision of hell dominated by a Devil with a blazing sixgun instead of a pitchfork, a raging Lucifer with the preacher's face.

The preacher exulted. No more doubts or uncertainties now. Here in his quiet room in the deep night, he knew the quest was finally at an end.

Yet it was astonishing how close he'd come to not going to spy on the newsman's house tonight. He'd done it before; he'd spied on all three, interrogated their friends and enemies, examined old council records and haunted the library searching for facts to back up his suspicions.

Whatever he'd thus gained had been flimsy at best. But tonight the whim that had driven him to go conceal himself in the smithy and spy one more time on the newsman's house had delivered solid gold.

For the very first time he'd confirmed his suspects conclaved together and by night. And the chance intrusion of that damned blacksmith had simply set the seal upon the whole thing. The harridan witness at his brother's death-scene had identified three men bending over the body: 'tallish, youngish, well-dressed.' The fourth man had been shadowy but she imagined him to have been older and heavier. Flanagan to a T!

He leaned forward in his chair to study his image in the bureau looking-glass. The face that stared back was seamed, savage and pale tonight, emphasizing the black glitter of his stare beneath hooked brows.

But there were other differences tonight. The nose appeared pushed to one side. There was a deep gash in the lower lip and the left earlobe was swollen and discolored.

He fingered a lower tooth and it moved.

He'd never fought a blacksmith before. Plain-looking, plain-spoken Flanagan was a powerhouse with grit in his gizzard.

And also one of them!

He rose to cross the room and stretched out upon the hard and narrow bunk against the wall. He prayed to his dead brother and promised his hour of retribution was at hand. Soon he slept, his breathing the sound the wind makes blowing through an empty skull.

'I believe we're winning, Ash,' Rand Malleroy said with a grin. 'Doone tried to come in earlier, but my doormen ganged up on him, as instructed. Of course he started raising hell, then I showed up and warned him

I'd call Wes and charge him with affray and disturbing the peace if he didn't leave. He was black in the face when he left, as he likes nothing better than to swagger into a saloon and then use it as a forum to attack people like me and give us merry hell.'

Carmody folded his arms and nodded.

'He came into the office complaining about the charge I made in Saturday's edition about the way he's holding the Crackers back by insisting they only seek work with employers he approves of. He got so angry that at one stage he started to say something about Kentucky and the wagon train, then broke off real sharp.' He nodded soberly. 'But at least that proves beyond any doubt that our notions about him and why he came, weigh up. I guess you could just about wager your last dollar now that he had some connection with that dead prospector . . .'

'They never did find out his name, did they?'

'No, and never will now, I guess. Well, better be off. What's on for you tonight, Rand?'

'Nothing in particular.' The saloonman grinned easily. 'Glad you dropped by, Ash. One good thing about us figuring Doone's game, we don't have to go round pretending we're not pards any longer.'

'You're right. Well, take it easy, Rand.'

Turning to go, Carmody idly noticed the pretty girl standing in the shadows by the piano. Thin and serious-looking, she was simply dressed and he sensed she was one of the Georgians from the poor side of town. He thought it unusual, in light of the fact that the preacher painted all saloons as nineteenth century Gomorrahs in the sermons he continued to feed them from his slaughterhouse pulpit.

As he passed out through the batwings, his friend was kicking his office door closed and taking the Georgian girl in his arms.

It had been going on for some time although only a handful of Two Bits personnel were aware of it. Malleroy had sworn his staff to secrecy about the affair, primarily to shield the girl from the preacher's wrath, but secondarily due to the fact that she was cheating on her boyfriend, a hard-eyed young Cracker with a reputation for violence.

With the lamps turned low, the lovers were toasting one another in champagne when the side door burst open and Ike Bacon burst in. He was drunk, he carried a sidearm, his girl was only half-dressed.

She screamed: 'No, Ike!' as he pulled his piece and came lunging across the room. Malleroy dived for his desk, ducked swiftly as the rusted .44 beat heavy thunder through the room. His drawer was opened and his hand closed over the little gambler's two-shot. He gasped as a second shot furrowed his arm. He steadied his grip and fired at point-blank range as the maddened man loomed over him.

The girl was still screaming when the case-keeper rushed in to see the ceiling splattered with blood and brains.

The judge weighed up the evidence and didn't hesitate to give his finding then and there:

Death occasioned by gunshot wound fired by

saloonkeeper Malleroy at the deceased in self-defense.

Case dismissed!

'When they come to take me down Glory Road,
Lord let me be ready . . . ready . . .
Lord let me be ready!'

There was little harmony in the singing, but it was fervent and it was loud. Gaunt and bitter folk from the dry back hills of Georgia gave it all they had, while drunks and good old boys with gin in their voices did their best to keep up with them stanza by stanza.

The whitewashed Church of God boasted a bumper crowd tonight.

It would have been hard to find anybody who could genuinely say they'd cared for Ike Bacon; some were even relieved he was gone. But shiftless, brutal, drunken and immoral though Ike undoubtedly was, he'd been one of them, and had been cut down in his prime by a man who wore forty-dollar suits of clothes and was never seen inside a church from one year's end to another.

Self-defense? They would see what the preacher had to say about that!

The advertisements had ensured a full house tonight. The posters, printed in large black type upon sheets of stiff yellow poster paper by the *Western Globe* and distributed widely around town, left nobody in any doubt concerning the theme:

Wake Up Wagontown!

Do not believe what you are told concerning the foul murder of Brother Ike Bacon. Come and hear the truth – if you have the courage to face it.
8 p.m. Wagontown Church Of God
Come one, come all!

CHAPTER 10

LET THE
DYING BEGIN

Sundown.

Ash Carmody touched a vesta to a short six and drew deeply as he stood watching the farm family trundle by in their battered wagon.

They were heading for the west side of town along with all the others, he realized. It was still half an hour short of eight o'clock, yet by his guess the preacher's church must be close to packed out already.

He'd not expected this even though well aware that Bacon had been a popular figure in the eyes of many of the poor and underprivileged. And it was no secret that the preacher had been on the streets day and night whipping up sentiment against 'the powerful and godless' – meaning the rich of Wagontown as opposed to the ragged poor. Yet he had not realized resentment ran so deep until right now.

'Lies-peddlin' bastard!'

The taunt came from a group of youths passing by in the gloom. It was followed by the clatter of a rock fired in his direction.

He was still staring after the receding pack when he saw Shelby and the Reverend Middleton emerge from a side street.

The first thing he noticed was that the lawman toted a Winchester in the crook of his arm.

He stepped down in the street and walked out to join them.

'What the hell is going on, Wes?' he demanded.

'You mean who, not what, Ash,' Shelby growled. He drew to a halt and put a hard eye upon a ragged couple heading in the same direction as the mob. 'Doone's got them worked up to a pitch already, and his damned service hasn't even started yet. I've been busy since sundown just trying to keep a lid on things. Mr Middleton's been doing what he can to help, but it's still not looking good.'

'The man is spreading all sorts of lies about how Ike Bacon died,' said Middleton, the quietly spoken little Easterner who'd already lost half his congregation to the fire-and-brimstone Church of God. 'Do you realize he's trying to incriminate you in that tragedy along with Sheriff Shelby, Ash?'

Carmody nodded grimly. He'd heard it but hadn't believed it. Maybe he'd had his head in the sand. He knew for sure he'd seriously underestimated the preacher's ability to exert power and influence over ever-growing numbers of hard-luckers in the town in the days since Bacon's death.

It seemed now that Doone had been preaching a virulent brand of us-against-them theology down at the slaughterhouse all along. But it had taken a shooting and a court hearing to give the whole movement a focal point centered upon their sense of outrage.

Overnight it seemed that wild Ike Bacon had been transformed into some kind of saint, with the preacher leading the campaign for his deification.

'We can't let this go on,' he opined as yet another straggle of men and women in drab clothing hurried on by. They glared back sullenly before eventually turning down the street leading to the slaughterhouse. He nodded to Wes. 'Anyway, I've got an editorial ready for tomorrow's edition that supports the judge's finding and where I call for common sense and an end to this hysteria, if that's all it is.'

Shelby clapped him on the shoulder.

'Good man, Ash. And the reverend here is holding a special service for Bacon at the real church tomorrow, and as well will be calling for calm and order.'

The lawman glanced around and adjusted the angle of his rifle.

'In the meantime I'd better get down there to the slaughterhouse, make sure things don't get out of hand. I'm not having any riots in my town.'

'You taking your deputies with you, Wes?'

Shelby shook his head.

'I've already got them out patrolling the streets.'

He nodded soberly. 'I guess I'd have to say this is the uneasiest night I've seen since pinning on this badge.'

'I'll accompany you, Sheriff,' Middleton offered. 'I must say I admire the preacher's fervour but I certainly don't agree with his extreme views.'

Carmody stood on the plankwalk watching them go. He rubbed the back of his neck as a cloud drifted across the face of the moon hanging over Front Street. For a long moment he was alone and for some reason began to feel a chill on this warm night.

The preacher sat alone in the vestry, listening to the ever-swelling buzz of noise from the other side of the thin walls. He'd just instructed Kelp to get busy with the preliminary prayers. He sat motionless with long hands folded in his lap, yet there was an air of leashed power and suppressed excitement about him that seemed to permeate his every lean inch.

This was exceeding all his expectations.

As usual, the Crackers had arrived early as they did every meeting, packing the front benches. The ragged poor formed the obsessive nucleus of all his gatherings. They had travelled hundreds upon hundreds of miles westward in the expectation of a brave new world, only to find here exactly what they had left behind in Georgia, Tennessee and the Carolinas. Amidst the poverty and rejection just one man offered them hope and spoke their language. The preacher. He alone understood the anger and pain they felt as the echoing whitewashed room was rapidly filled by what looked like the entire loser population of the city on the plains.

And enveloping them all, whether Georgian, businessman, cowboy, child or dancehall girl, was an air of outrage and anticipation.

The preacher was thanking Ike Bacon from the bottom of his heart.

When he'd set out to eulogize the reckless young Cracker who'd been blasted to death at the Two-Bits saloon, the preacher had hoped to make some capital out of it. Yet he'd succeeded beyond his hopes. Overnight, Bacon was transformed from hell-raiser to a wide-eyed innocent blown away in his prime by a slick and uppity outsider who called judges and lawmen his friends.

Doone had been pandering increasingly to his congregation's prejudices and hatreds ever since the moment he grew convinced that the killer he'd hunted for so long was here in Wagontown.

Without his converts and followers, he would be a single man pitched against an unknown enemy strength. With them he would have the strength to exact whatever vengeance would be called for. He referred to them as his 'sainted poor'. In his dark mind they were cannon fodder, if needed.

It had been one bum's violent death that signalled to Doone that his moment had arrived. For more than a year and a half he'd had to control his murderous impatience as he sought the vital clue, the scent and the moment that would lead him to the guilty.

The time was now!

It was time to unleash the dogs of violence and exact his revenge ... to pacify his hunger for final retribution that had been gnawing at his insides for almost two years.

Ever since that evil day in Cairo.

In his past lay the death of his father – gunned down by Ethan Doone in one of his early mad rages. Years of estrangement from his only sibling had been the result. Yet during those years his passion for violence had been harnessed in tandem with his consuming love of his God.

Soon he was killing less and preaching more. His new vocation opened up new vistas, and yet his past sins continued to haunt him. The only man who might forgive him, his brother, was lost in the wilderness someplace searching for gold.

Then came the letter from nowhere. Brother Abel had finally made his strike and now declared himself to be all through with prospecting and the sinful life. Abel Doone wished only to be redeemed and reunited with his elder brother and forgive him for his father's death, now that Ethan had found the Lord. He now wanted Ethan to lead him down the path of salvation.

The plans were made to meet up in Cairo and make use of Abel's riches to build a mighty temple to the Lord someplace in the snowy West.

Their future was bathed in a golden glow – yet was destined never to be fulfilled. An attack by thieves, a knife-fight to the death in an unnamed riverside street in Cairo had denied him absolution for ever.

Leaving nothing for the surviving brother but revenge, revenge, revenge. . . .

'Preacher!'

He blinked and started.

'What . . . ?' He stared up to see Kelp standing before him. Cruel and twisted images faded from his eyes. 'Yes, what is it, man?'

'They're ready, Preacher.'

He rose and stood tall, eyes afire. 'And so am I, acolyte, so am I. Lead the way!'

He strode into the white room to thunderous applause and delivered his fiercest and fieriest sermon ever against their mutual and collective 'enemies'.

Those rich, arrogant and educated citizens who denied them equality, who confined them to fringe-dwelling in shanty towns while they lived in robbers' castles uptown.

Who murdered their brothers and called it justice!

When it was over, he didn't have to tell his wild-eyed congregation what must be done. They told him.

'You're standing by the window again, darling.'

Carmody turned.

'Huh? Oh, yeah, I guess I was.'

Ruth smiled up at him.

'Why don't you put on your jacket and go down to Front Street? You'll be fidgety all night if you don't,

145

wondering what's going on. I'll be fine.'

He shook his head. Had he been sure of her safety he would be down there now seeing what all the fuss was about, examining the town's mood, most likely looking up Wes and Rand.

But he knew he wouldn't leave. The fact that the preacher had been recently caught spying on the house from directly across the street had added a hint of personal danger not present before.

'I've a better notion,' he said with a grin. 'I'll go make some coffee.'

'Everything will be all right, Ash. You'll see.'

'Sure,' he said, going out. 'Everything will be just fine.' And added under his breath: 'I hope.'

The first whiff of trouble reached the Two-Bits when a porch loafer blundered through the batwings to announce that a mob was heading down Front.

Shelby and Malleroy were taking a drink in the private bar. They set their glasses down and hurried out.

'There's the dirty murderer!' a hoarse voice shouted from the heart of the marchers.

'Doone's holy-rollers!' Shelby said angrily. 'By hell, I'll soon put a stop to this.'

'Take it easy,' Malleroy urged. 'They look mean.'

'I'll show them who's mean.'

The lawman stepped out into the street as the mob first slowed, then halted. He set out to address them but they were past that. Their clamor drowned him out and the surge forward began again. He drew his gun and drilled a shot into the sky. The uproar faded as they faltered. He was about to continue when a flung stone arced out of the gloom of an adjacent alley and thudded hard against the side of his head. His hat spilling to the roadway, the lawman dropped to his knees, then rolled onto his back, bleeding and dazed.

An awed silence fell. Raging as they had been, the sea of faces was suddenly fearful as they looked to the towering figure in black for guidance. Doone strode forward to confront the saloonman from behind an accusing finger.

'Murderer!'

Malleroy stared in disbelief. He knew many of the faces in the mob, yet they were wearing looks he'd never seen before. They were strangers as they began shouting: 'Ike, Ike! He killed Ike!'

'Will I put a shot over their heads, Rand?' asked his dealer at his elbow.

'No, it'd only make them worse,' he said. He lifted his voice. 'Doone, what in Hades do you think you're about?'

Before the preacher could answer, a hoarse shout sounded from the saloon. 'Fire!'

Malleroy rushed back into the saloon, his face going a dead white. Thin tongues of flame were visible towards the scullery at the rear. As he stood gaping, a drape caught alight and a snake of flame flickered from the roof. With a choked-off curse he rushed back out front to find the mob closing in.

'Doone!' he raged. 'You filthy fake! This is all your

stinking work. A man ought to kill you for it!'

Doone flicked the panel of his coat behind his Colt butt. His face was demonic. 'As you also killed our beloved brother Ike, purveyor of filth? It is I who should kill you – murderer!'

'Murderer?'

'Murderer!' echoed the mob.

'You . . . you told them that, Doone?'

'I did, as that is what you are. You see, the girl confessed the truth, Malleroy. Confessed it to me as she had not dared do before your venal judge. And now you shall pay the supreme price.'

In that instant, stamped clear upon Doone's face and in the surging sea of the mob, Malleroy saw what this really was. Everything in this menacing scene had been planned and intended, by Doone. And now with flames behind him and a mob before him there was only one possible way out.

'Then draw, you insane son of a bitch!' he roared. 'I will kill you for this!'

Doone's gun leapt and crashed before Malleroy's weapon reached firing level. The bullet drove the saloonkeeper backwards and his gun exploded, hammering a bullet into the porch boards. The preacher's gun churned once more and Malleroy fell back against the wall and lay still. The dealer leveled his weapon at the towering figure of the Preacher, who triggered once more to slam the man back clutching a bloodied shoulder. The shotgun dropped with a clatter. Slowly and majestically, Doone mounted the porch steps and stared down at Malleroy's body.

'It was the Lord's will, brothers and sisters. He has exacted His vengeance though us.' Yet even as he spoke, the question turned over in his tortuous mind: was he really the one?

In his self-obsession and triumph, he didn't realize the crowd behind him had fallen totally silent. They could not take their eyes off the dead saloon-keeper.

The preacher's face darkened ominously. 'You are going to do what, sir?'

'You heard,' Shelby snarled. 'I am closing you down. I've let you have your head ever since you came here, and that was a mistake. By simply allowing you to set up down there and spew out your bile and hate, I was party to the death of a man worth a hundred of you. After what happened last night I'm decreeing that those meetings constitute a threat to law and order. They're finished. You are finished!'

'You have heard of freedom of worship, I take it, lawman?'

Shelby massaged his heavily strapped head and came around his desk. He held the sixgun he'd confiscated from Doone the previous night. He handed it across, barrel first.

'Maybe you should be honest with yourself and make your living with this . . . this stinking thing and leave the Bible alone. You are, after all, just a dirty cheap gunslinger. A cold-blooded butchering bastard, certainly not any kind of man of God.'

'You sound like your friend, Carmody. I read his editorial this morning. The three of you, Carmody,

Malleroy – yourself – all speak with one voice. And why would that be, do you wonder? Would it have anything to do with . . .'

The preacher broke off abruptly and quit the office. He had suddenly and obsessively realized that he had to be sure that his reasoning in identifying Malleroy as the guilty one had been sound.

Attorney Erskine was puzzled.

'Why, yes, the late Mr Malleroy was indeed a client of mine, as you suggest, er . . . Preacher. Why do you ask?'

'I am stricken with remorse, sir. I am a man of the Word, not a man of the gun.' The tall figure leaned forward. 'You see, it has come to my ears that the late Mr Malleroy died in dire financial straits, that he owed his staff, the bank, everyone. If this is the case I would like to make restitution and also see that the poor fellow receives a decent burial.'

'Why, that is very magnanimous of you, sir,' the attorney said warily. 'Generous, but unnecessary. As his attorney and manager of his business affairs, I can assure you that the late Mr Malleroy was very much solvent and anything but broke, as you suggest.'

The preacher's eyes glittered as he leaned forward. 'He arrived here with gold, did he not?' He was thinking of the gold stolen from his murdered brother.

The man frowned.

'Gold? Not at all.'

'You're lying!'

Erskine flushed. 'How dare you, sir!'

'Forgive me. It was a terrible thing . . . forced to defend myself against this man. It's just that I was certain it was gold that enabled the deceased to buy the biggest saloon in Wagontown for cash and—'

The attorney rose. 'I don't have to do this, but seeing as you are so obviously misinformed about my late client, I feel I should set you straight. Mr Malleroy's father died several months after he arrived here, and Mr Mallerory was sole beneficiary of the will. That was the source of his affluence. And now if you will excuse me, sir . . . ?'

Back on the street, Doone paused and passed a trembling hand across his brow. He'd been so sure! Moments later he straightened and began to walk slowly westward. Malleroy still might have been the Cairo knife murderer. But what if he wasn't? Dare he allow his brother's true killer escape justice?

By the time he reached the first corner his dark mind was focusing on Wes Shelby and Ash Carmody. The fire that burned in him had not been quenched after all.

Ruth Carmody carried a tray laden with coffee-cups into the parlor where her husband sat talking with Reverend Middleton and Wes Shelby.

The mood was somber, the talk ranging over past good times shared with Rand Malleroy, the dead man's hopes and aspirations for the future, none of which would be realized now.

Ruth Carmody was pleased to have the reverend's

company today. She knew just how enraged her husband and the sheriff were about the killing. Of course she knew that neither would even think of taking reprisal action against Preacher Ethan Doone. But Middleton's calming presence and good words were plainly proving beneficial to both.

So they drank their coffee and smoked cigars, and looking out the windows saw that it was just another bright day in Kansas which in no way reflected the darkness that engulfed them today, and might continue to do so for a long time.

Rand had been little more than a casual acquaintance when they'd reached the Mississippi. But he'd become a friend during their time in Wagontown.

Vale, friend.

Shelby glanced at his watch and rose with a sigh.

'Time I got back to the office. I don't like to leave the boys alone too long on a day like this.'

As if on cue, there came a knock on the door. When Ruth attended it, Deputy Vinn Tyler stood there, hat in hand.

'What is it?' Shelby asked as she showed the man in.

'You ain't gonna believe this, Sheriff.'

'What?'

'It's about him, Sheriff. That dirty, butchering fake of a preacher. The word's around he's callin' another meetin' for tonight.'

Shelby paled. 'Are you sure of that, Vinn?'

'I figured it had to be wrong, Sheriff. But I met that creepin' Kelp on the street, and without battin' an eye he told me about it hisself. Figgered you should know.'

After a long moment's silence, Carmody said:

'Looks like he's calling your bluff, Wes.'

'He'll wish he hadn't,' the sheriff said grimly. He took down his hat and thanked Ruth for her hospitality. He paused for a grim last word. 'I thought Doone would be smarter than that. I banned any more meetings, so he's in contempt of the law. I can jail him for that. I will.'

'Be careful, Wes,' Ash counselled.

'No,' the lawman said grimly, striding out. 'It's that bloody-handed fake that should take care.'

The preacher's expression was stunned as he surveyed the meager attendance. He bent a quizzical stare on the ubiquitous Kelp, who spread pale hands.

'They're too scared to roll up, Preacher. The sheriff warned them against any more meetings, and I guess they took it to heart.'

The man was lying in his teeth. There was good reason why attendance had plummeted from 200 to barely twenty, and it had little to do with anybody being scared. What the poor, the luckless and the downtrodden were suffering from tonight was disillusionment on a massive scale. They had come to idolize the preacherman for his eloquence, tolerated his aggression as showmanship. But the slaughter of a townsman had ripped the blinkers from their eyes, and only the true die-hards and hardest haters were here tonight.

Doone clamped his lips tight.

'Never mind. These true few have come to hear the Blessed Saviour's words, and hear them they shall. The organ if you will, Mr Kelp.'

He was well into his sermon when the doors swung inward with a bang and Sheriff Shelby stood there with the light behind him. The Church of God fell silent as the tall figure in the pulpit closed his Bible with a snap.

'Doone, you are under arrest!'

'You're overstepping yourself, Sheriff. This is the Lord's house.'

'I won't tell you again, Doone. Come down off there. You are accompanying me to the jailhouse.'

'Afraid not, sir.'

Calmly, deliberately, the preacher quit the pulpit and moved to stand on the altar's edge, his height seemingly enhanced by the light of fluttering candles.

'Not another step, I warn you, lawman!' He flicked the panel of his coat and the deadly black gun was there for all to see, to every wide-eyed worshipper.

Coming forward, Shelby propped.

'You are defying me . . . in this place?'

'You chose the place, sir.' Behind his locked features, the preacher's brain was raging. Following the revelation on Malleroy's wealth he had convinced himself that Shelby, the man of the gun, had to be his brother's killer. Believed it because he wanted to believe. He raised his chin. 'You are not arresting me, lawdog!'

'I'm going to draw my gun, Doone. If you resist I'll shoot you.'

Worshippers were diving for the floor when they saw the red light flare in the preacher's eyes.

His big hand wrapped around gun-handle, Wes Shelby swayed a little then brought the Colt whipping up. In that shaved tip-end of a moment, Doone cleared his weapon and fired. One shot. The bullet passed clear through the sheriff's chest and struck a ragged child in the very back row. Wes Shelby began staggering towards the smoke-wreathed figure before him. He fell on his back with blood streaming from his chest.

People were screaming and weeping but Doone paid no heed as he dropped to one knee at the dying man's side. His smile of triumph was hideously inappropriate.

'Butchering bastard!' Shelby gasped.

'I am the avenger of the sacred dead,' Doone corrected. 'You gave my poor brother death in Cairo, but I offer you eternal life with our Blessed Lord if you will but confess your terrible sin.'

Confusion contorted the dying lawman's features.

'Are you talking about that prospector? You bloody fool! He was dead when we reached him. He'd been killed and robbed—'

'Liar!' Doone raged, seizing him by the vest. 'To lie on your very death bed is . . .'

He heard the death rattle. He let the body drop. His face was haggard with disbelief. He knew from wide experience gained over a violent lifetime that no man will die with a lie on his lips.

He'd erred again!

Not Malleroy. Not Shelby. Then it had to be . . .

He slowly realized that people were calling to him, women weeping. There was angry shouting. He blinked and stared around. They were carrying the wounded child towards him, tears streaming down careworn faces. Still others had fallen away, clustering along the whitewashed walls as though terrified by what they'd seen.

'Please, Preacher,' the mother cried. 'My little one . . .'

'Out of my way!' he almost shouted. He kicked the dead man's legs out of his path, then shoved a man who got in his way. 'Can't you see I must be about my Father's work? The guilty will not survive this night!'

They flinched away from him as he went striding for the doors. They were shocked, fearful, and something more. In their eyes, their pale faces, there was a rushing light of understanding to which they had been been blinded before. It was as if they were seeing the real Preacher Doone for the very first time . . . feeling suddenly the first dark flickerings of rage . . . and hate.

Ruth Carmody's eyes were wide with fear. 'Ash, what on earth are you doing? You . . . you've never worn a gun. You can't be thinking of . . . of fighting this monster. He'll kill you the way he killed Rand and Wes. Good God! You've just heard the deputies say they're too afraid to stand against such a butcher. You're going to commit suicide!'

Carmody finished buckling on the revolver he'd never expected to use. He realized everything his wife was saying made sense. If some miracle didn't save him, the preacher would show up soon and blow him to hell. But there was no time to run. The deputies had warned that the preacher was already on his way, trailed by what appeared to be an angry mob of Crackers.

And nothing could stop him. Wes had been Wagontown's top gunhand, but the Crackers from the Church of God had told the lawmen Doone had out-drawn Shelby and cut him down without his getting a single shot away.

He was ready.

He moved to kiss his wife goodbye but she drew back in horror and anger.

'Then go ahead!' she cried. 'Be a hero and kill yourself, if that is what you must do. Die if you want!'

He glimpsed shadowy figures on the street as he stepped outside. He moved through the gateway like a man in a trance and slowly became aware of the tall silhouette standing in the shadows of the smithy across the wide roadway.

His mouth went dry. He licked his lips and eased the .45 in its leather. His gaze swept the scene which seemed unreal to his gaze, neighbors . . . a swelling number of Crackers, strangely silent . . . more onlookers coming from the town center in a hurry as though afraid they might miss something.

The tall man detached from the smithy and started towards him.

The deputies had told him that Doone had delayed for several minutes in the central block to inform the lawmen of his intentions and to warn them of the same fate should they attempt to stop him. Hence the swelling throng, some plainly excited, others horrified . . . the growing swarm of Crackers strangely silent where he expected them to be urging their spiritual leader on.

The preacher halted in the center of the street, hatless, long hair stirring in the night wind.

'You slew my brother in Cairo and I've been hunting you every hour since, Carmody.'

'We didn't kill that man. He was dead when we found him!' the voice of Flanagan declared from amongst the ever swelling crowd of Crackers, which seemed to be drawing closer now. 'I was there too, Doone. Your brother was dead with a knife in his chest. He'd been robbed and killed. We heard later they never caught the killer or saw the gold ag—'

'Silence, liar!' The preacher's right hand hung by his side. 'Carmody, prepare to meet thy Maker—'

'He shot the child!' a Cracker woman suddenly shrieked from the surging crowd. 'He killed the sheriff as you would a beast . . . and he shot the little girl. . . .'

A pause, then: 'Murderer.' And, 'False prophet! Instrument of the devil!'

'He is the devil!'

'And the devil must die!'

In an instant the gathering crowd of Crackers seemed transformed into a raging mob. On every hand now there were angry faces, cheated faces, the faces of victims used, deceived and exploited just one more time . . . and all in the name of God.

Stunned, disbelieving, Carmody tried to focus on Doone and thus saw the missile sail from the crowd, something dark and heavy looking. It struck the towering figure in the middle of the back. Doone lurched forward, his mouth agape in agony. A shrewish woman screamed in triumph and another at her side wept:

'He could have slain our little boy. Hamish, don't you be lettin' him harm any other innocents!'

The child's burly father came raging from the mob. Somehow Doone straightened, his big black gun rising slowly, his face alive with murderous intent as the mob came rushing forward.

'Back!' he roared, gun in hand, triggering now. 'How dare you menace the bringer of the Word. How—'

In one savage surging moment he was down and outraged faces encircled him, striking murderously at the one man they had trusted, now revealed as yet another enemy in their long quest for the Promised Land.

For a moment the preacher's head and shoulders reared out up of the surging human sea. Then a long blade glinted in the light and struck home. The giant figure crashed to earth and didn't move, the fanning cloud of his hair concealing his dead face.

While Ash Carmody toiled at his desk to complete his

issue-long story on Cairo, a long-ago crime, two fine friends and Preacher Doone and his great evil – his wife stood behind him resting her hand on his shoulder. Elsewhere another citizen of Wagontown was also pondering and 'searching for the right words'.

Frowning over the slab of rough board that would form the preacher's headboard in the dishonored Stranger's Ground in the wood behind the cemetery, the undertaker conceived and rejected a dozen possibilities.

It wasn't until his wife called him to supper that inspiration came, and he quickly went to work with hammer and chisel.

He was through by the time his good lady summoned him the second time. He set down his tools and left the room as the last rays of sunset probed beneath the window blind. A bar of light briefly fell across the inscription, illuminating them as though the letters were etched in fire. Just three simple words:

God Forgive Him